PAGE PUBLISHING, INC.
Conneaut Lake, PA

First originally published by Page Publishing 2021

ISBN 978-1-6624-2189-1 (hc)
ISBN 978-1-6624-2190-7 (digital)

Printed in the United States of America

WITCHWOOD
FOREST

DEVIL JAMES

To all the early on stoned, lost, wasted, misunderstood,
and pissed-off misfits and outcasts of society
(A dark curse we have endured)

PREFACE

To MY DEAR readers, please remember this when you read my stoner stories of active creative imagination, which paint pictures of every emotion and thought in demented detail, that whatever roller coaster of ups and downs of emotions and thoughts that most of us do our best to push back down within the lost, empty chambers of our cold hearts, thoughts we choose to never think or face by fading out the things we do not want to think or remember by pushing them into the darkest loneliest emptiest places in our confused, bewildered, shocked, and numb minds because we are afraid of those thoughts and feelings and what they may create or what they might find, I take out this time to remind all my dear loyal readers and loved ones to never forget that these books and stories are meant to do just that—to expand our minds by picking the scabs off suppressed memories and facing the dreadful thoughts we may be afraid to think or face these emotions that we may not want to feel because it may take us to a dark or lonely place.

Please remember I am an artist, a musician, and a writer. These artistic forms of expression are an outlet for my own self, a therapeutic, unique weird way from the strange ways, I think, and the crazy things I say and write are in my own style of genre or with some influence "gonzo style" by the infamous cult hero writer Hunter S. Thompson. My other writer influence was my favorite, dear Edgar Alan Poe, for his romantic dark side expressionism. These 2 famous authors were just two of about six of my favorite poets and authors that have inspired me, and in that way, maybe perhaps they rubbed off in small unknown ways into my own creative writings and imaginations. Hunter committed suicide by shooting himself in the head, Edgar drank himself to death and was a heavy drug abuser whose actual death is shrouded in mystery.

In short, the purpose of this preface is having deep love and compassion in my heart for not just my friends, my family, my faithful fans of my oil paintings, and loyal readers who love my books and my unique style. I have lived my life with mental illnesses and deep major depression disorder, so I want to be a beacon for each and every one of you. I want to be your shooting star in the dark, dreary, lonely night. I want to be your steady lighthouse on the rocky ocean shore in the middle of a foggy dark thunderstorm. I want to be your own source of inspiration in a not-so-perfect world. I want to remind you all that the yin-yang of good and bad is in everything, that although this can be a tough cruel world, it is also equally beautiful, and although you may not be perfect and may suffer from despair, sorrow, depression, or mental illness, it's okay to shine bright as the unique person you are and to keep fighting and keep rolling with the punches and keep getting up every day to face the next weird, strange, peculiar yet wonderful world we all live in.

I want to remind you all that life is not fair or perfect, and none of us are perfect. I want to remind you it's not only okay to cry, but that I encourage it by facing all those thoughts and feelings that haunt us, the ones we try to suppress and trick ourselves to forget. So never give up or give in to the evil in the world. Never ignore it or pretend it's not there. In the spirit of it is what it is, embrace everything in this world and everything within our hearts and minds for what they really are. Thank you for reading my books. I hope they touch you, motivate you, heal you, inspire you, set you free, and open doors in your heart and in your minds.

THERE WAS A place long forgotten that stood in solitude, a sacred old place where the howling winds fall still in eerie silence, a place of legends and lore. This is the story of Witch Wood Forest.

I start up my old black Buick with my skeleton driving gloves on. Feeling the squeeze of lovesick depression of a lonely outcast, I prepare to let the spirits that plague and stain me as parasites as they once again take over, pushing them into the old engine like a possessed machine from a demented version of Christine from hell. Revving the engine as to call the devil himself to ride along on what the local stoners and freaks used to call hell rides (and for good reason), I rarely ever showed any living soul this "gift" of my private personal tormenting curse of parasitic demons, because what few fellow "pals" from an antisocial natural loner as myself who was fortunate to go on a midnight booze cruise with me and to witness me letting my car drive itself would never look at me the same, which only saddened me more deeply and increased my deep rooted depression. What I looked as a unique gift of taming the demons and beasts, others would see in fear and dread and soon after would always distance themselves from me. With that being said, fuck 'em. This story isn't about them anyway; it's a dark love story from a broken heart from a loner for life doomed to live a loner life and die alone in some miserable dark hour on a drug overdose or, even worse, a fucking bullet by a dirty gun in the fucking head by my own hands, which is why hell rides were important to me.

They called back the old timey spirits that know my pain all too well. Old-time black magic, baby, so fuck running with the devil, I was going to entertain Lucifer while I entertained myself with a fifth of whiskey, some of the devil's weed, and some good haunting stoner doom metal blasting out the speakers. Whoever feels intently exactly what I mean may have the power to even call on my spirit someday once I am dead and gone. Just remember that when one pushes the limits where life meets the edge of death (in the spirit of do as I say and not as I do), what you hold in your hands is your own fate, and for that you must be prepared to face the consequences of your own actions—that is, unless you're like me, so heartbroken and dismally depressed that you know longer giveth a fucketh.

In that spirit, before I take you any further into this haunting tale of despair, loneliness, and heartbreak, let me just clear my thoughts with a "fuck the world." If that don't sit right with you, then fuck you. Stop reading, and go fuck yourself. My pain has festered into something far more dangerous than a typical suicidal or homicidal frustration. Mine is more ancient and ageless in the key of "fuck off." With that being said, for all I know, I may be unknowingly cursing you by writing this tormenting truth among the big windy stories that camouflage its dreadful existence.

I gunned the engine, speeding out of town over the rolling hills of the old blacktop country roads just far enough to see the town disappear into the rearview mirror and the environment easing into surreal relaxing cornfields and forests—the code to knowing it was safe enough to crack open the fifth of Jack Daniels and take a bittersweet satisfying burning swig, as the gulp of sour mash whiskey gratefully burned down to my belly and rewarded my brain with the crazy cracker redneck buzz of a country road booze cruise from hell that always delivers. Gets me where I'm trying to go *every time*. I need the numbing buzz to mask all the physical pain and heart-wrenching depression to be able to think and remember and recall, or I will never be able to take you somewhere else, someplace far back in a distant reminiscing, past all this rage and hate, sadness and depression.

I leaned back the car seat and let go of the steering wheel as the old spirits in the old machine took over for me, always keeping not just a watchful eye but a heart full of constant presence in the moment. I felt empathy for my spirit drivers and my ghost machine on four wheels, always slowly picking apart any old recipe for disaster and making it my own with my enchanting ingredients of magic meets mayhem and the dark thrill of it all.

This story isn't about all the local wild cards, in and out convicts, potential satanic serial killers, or the crazy bikers who cruise these haunted back roads shooting stray cats to skin 'em and cut off their heads to add to their cat skull collection. This is a story that separates a tortured soul like myself from the crazed monsters that can't see past their own rage and hurt for whatever reasons. I am proud to say that despite my hurt and anger, I am still a compassionate, caring human being, just a wounded one who prefers my own dark solitude. Even when these monstrous, heartless "human beings" become obsessed with me in their own cautious stalking ways, I still manage to keep them at a safe distance or, even better yet, out of sight and company in general, preferring the company of the dead, the lost spirits, and the ghosts of the past over any human companionship. It's all about the kind of lessons in this life that sometimes do not even challenge the morality in any of us until we have left these human lives behind and enter into the oblivious unknown of the beyond...beyond the grave.

As I cruise these old familiar twisted curved blacktopped country roads through miles of barren forests and combinations of cornfields and soybean fields, I felt the burning, comforting sting of the Jack Daniels reward my brain and general condition in a grateful buzz that delivered a careless, carefree attitude that society, city living, and socializing in general seems to rob and drain from the natural energy we as all people are supposed to have but are too blinded by society's meaningless bullshit to notice we are trading in our drive for life and the energy and interest to keep us all going with dismal, dreary depression, apathy, and self-defeat in the forms of stressful low self-esteem that come in waves of loss of interest, loss of excitement and curiosity, and loss of natural joy of life in general. The joy of simply being alive should greet us all every precious morning we open our eyes and greet a brand-new day, but the weight and squeeze of this tough old cruel world is no different to me than being helplessly caught in the unseen constricting coils of a giant hungry anaconda or python who has us all in the tightening, squeezing coils of death, slowly squeezing a little tighter each time we exhale every precious breath, to only have every exhale robbed from us replaced with the countdown of demising inhales, each smaller and more little than the one before until we are lifeless limp cold corpses on the cold tables of the funeral parlors back rooms, a fading distant image in the rounded reflection of the hazy cataract eyes of the mortician who knows the painful squeeze all too well.

Every minute of every second, we are slowly dying in the invisible coils of society's heartless cruelty of harsh judgments and lack of understanding, compassion, and sweet, gentle mercy that we are all slowly adapting to. This cold cruel world is eating us all alive, and the warmth of her smiles, her laughter, her caring advice of support and understanding were my warm rays of dawn's sunrise in the midst of all this hectic, chaotic jealous hatred. Her warmth from a radiant personality was just a wonderful part of the whole mesmerizing package that made her up. The warmth of her sweet, sexy body, her precious, loving beating heart would fill me with hope any and every time I was in her loving embrace, the arms of a human angel.

I felt the accelerator under my foot ease up as the brake pedal pushed down on its own with no help from me, my hands not on the wheel as the steering wheel slowly took the turn that led me to Witchwood's infamous gates of hell. I took another burning gulp of the oak barrel aged sour mash whiskey with my right arm and wiped the tears from my cheek with the left arm. Old life has a way about weighing us all down and stealing the pep and skip in your step and replacing it with dragging, shuffling feet slowly walking the plank to the bitter destination of dead-end demise.

The empty passenger seat and all the ghosts of those dear friends and beautiful lovers who would keep my spirit-driving ghost companions a secret while I pretended to drive old Bathory the black Buick on my own caused me to set the fifth of sour mash oak barrel whiskey in the empty seat beside me and recall in terrified tear-filled eyes all those precious souls who would honor me with their company in my own humble appreciation of all the absent kind smiles, joyful laughter, and rare tiny precious gifts of adoring women. The slow rolling cold tears trickle down my cheek as the certain souls of certain smiling faces stood out in my memory more than others, which brings you and I past the haunting pain of heart-aching painful rage and festering anger and into the true beginning of this unsettling tale—a story from the darkest corners of a torn and bruised, battered and shattered, patched up broken heart that no amount of sincerest apologies can bring back the old glory of the previous years of splendor, the strength, speed, and agility of restless enchanting youth gone with it. I placed my hand on the empty seat while the already half-empty fifth of whiskey slopped around on the beautiful, imperfect uneven roads of these old back-wood hillbilly country roads and stare at my skeleton gloved hands resting on that empty chair next to me while my beaten-up heart ached as I imagined her ghostly image in its place. Her heartwarming, beautiful silent empathy behind stoned eyes and a mischievous crooked stoner's smirk illuminated the kind of precious energy more powerful than even some of the sincerest words from the truest heart.

As the tears welled and built up the blinding flood, I must tell you now in sad lonely confessions that it is here past the Devil's Cut and beyond watchful eyes of weeping angels is where this tale of Witchwood Forest officially begins. So come take a seat next to me and sit beside me in good old Bathory, the black Buick, while lost and forgotten ghostly spirits drive us into my old stompin' grounds' places of legendary lore in my spirit machine as she calls back the spirits lost in time. Join me while I call back the spirit of the one I loved.

She was a diamond in the rough, in the almost endless sea of human beings of every and all kinds—the good, the bad, the ugly, the selfless compassionate, and selfish heartless. She was that rare shooting star so precious and different among the precious and different that even the most tortured souls of enduring the curse of extreme uniqueness would share her gratefully stoned smirks. She was a diamond in the dark abandoned bat-infested haunted coal mines, so unique in an eccentric abstract harmony that even if she took league with the darkness itself, the gods would take a deep concern of pity as they would pluck her from the cold dark fog themselves to dust her off and claim her among the divine. Even St. Michael was given the new title of forgiveness as an archangel, being the rarest to be released from Satan's cursed lot. Oh, how even in the darkest nights and within the darkest hours, how she would shine bright a natural energy that made the toughest, pickiest Valkyries take notice.

Old Bathory the Buick's dashboard lights grew dim a few times as if the spirits that kept it running on its own were tugging on my shirt sleeve to get my attention. I was so lost in my torn-shattered mind of depressing dementia that the Buick herself had to regain my attention to say in unspoken spiritual words, "We are here," and so, my dear reader and companion for the night, we have made it to destination Witchwood through the old-timey infamous gates of hell.

Welcome. As I thank you for staying with me this far, allow me to cautiously warn you, before you read on. We are *here*. We made it, and although unlike her (the one I so adore and long for), I know after riding along in a haunted and cursed car with a spirit of its own with a tortured, tormented soul like me, you will probably, just like the others who witnessed what most people slip into denial in believing, never look at me the same again. That is okay, because before I describe to you where I just took you, I need to prepare you and toughen you up, opening your heart and mind for this sacred dark place, for after you walk with me through the old forgotten bone yards of Witchwood Forest and weep tears of despair with me down along the banks of Devils Creek, you, too, will not only be forever changed in a never-the-same sense, but you will maybe even be strong enough to face the things that torment and torture kindred souls and plague once free-thinking creative imaginations from wandering wondering minds into the creeping dark plague of insecure, paranoid dementia. Perhaps you may even be able to face "them."

But for now, let me explain to you where we are at. Years ago, when we were just daring teenagers, we would venture out into this place, where the forest of Witchwood would separate old Devils Creek and surround the almost hidden and forgotten eighteenth-century cemeteries that age out there among the overgrown spiderwebbed weeds and the weathered and cracked broken old-timey headstones that marked the buried remains of a once living soul long forgotten. As you read these words into the sacred legendary hallowed grounds of Witchwood Forest, let it be known now before we dare go any further that as sure as those old weathered headstones crumble away by the ravages of time over lost forgotten souls that once lived and breathed like you and I, so shall you someday. Many long-lost moons and bitter cold seasons come and go before not a living soul walking this earth could recall your name or face, and such is the haunted time of forgotten places where the lost dead gather from beyond, listening in the eerie silence for any sign of the living. These woods have heard and seen things far stranger and darker than any veteran corner in the big city. Out here in Witchwood Forest is a gathering of legendary paranormal grounds that are more creepy and stranger than any tall tale of fiction from even the most active imagination. These places far out in between little hick towns and deep into winding, twisting mazes of old blacktop country roads are tales and history that are more creepy and heartbreaking than any story could conjure; however, certain events have been recited out here for that purpose alone—to conjure the old and the lost, the forgotten and the missed.

And in between these places of tears and fears are things even still more terrifying. Because Witchwood is just a part of a much bigger place of legend and lore and rich history of pagan rituals, black magic ceremony, and satanic mass. Not all locals call it Witchwood, although they know what it means and where it is at when you say the name. This place is steeped in such generations of mystery and paranormal that the cluster of haunted grounds that all hellishly connect each certain area to another gives it an even more sinister and well-known name—the gates of hell, infamous even in the days of our great-grandparents as a haunted cluster of connected lands that hold as much supernatural history and present-day paranormal energy as it does the endless tales of ghosts and black magic cults, sacrificial ceremonies, and the main subject of this heart-wrenching tale, tragedy, heartbreaking loss and haunting residual energy of innocent, adored lives ripped violently from this earth, leaving behind powerful emotions of sorrow, sadness, and despair.

Along the infamous gates of hell is the long twisted, muddy, murky little river with a deep strong underflow known as Devils Creek, a dark watered tiny river that winds and twists for miles through the remote sticks of Witchwood Forest and a few other neighboring woods. Among the infamous haunted grounds of the legendary gates of hell also hold other many endless myths of lore and creepy things that some hold more truth than others, and even a few of those are actually true to almost factual science, such as the infamous ley lines, or as some call 'em, the witch lines, a paranormal anomaly of residual energy that holds mysterious power, best described in the simplest way a land or earth version of the infamous Bermuda and devil's triangles. This old earth has land lines and water lines. They cut through multiverses and inner dimensions, and I feel that it is very important for me to explain to you this place to help paint a picture in your mind and maybe even get a sense of the eerie, dreadful feelings of impending doom that illuminate the whole area before I go on. Places like these are kept hush-hush and only frequently visited or mentioned by those who seek it and respect it or even fear it.

She will always be the main returning fixation of this story, and as I take you through these infamous haunted grounds and allow them to take over your wandering confused mind, I promise I will always bring you back to this tale's main obsession, which is *her*. She will come walking out of the cold lonely darkness in a pale mist of ectoplasms' drifting smoky fog to consume and embrace you and feed off your sorrows for all end of time, never to be seen again.

The ley lines cross along Devils Creek and some of Witchwood cemetery, creating what the native Americans would describe as the spirit world and what the modern Catholics back in town would refer to as a type of purgatory, where dimensions can hold you for a few hours, a few days, or endlessly as you correct all your flaws and your imperfections, never to hurt another living soul again. Once you reached true compassion and loving empathy, you will be released to leave with this feeling you battle within. Dreaming of a much simpler times, I would always take caution as I wandered Witchwood Forest in circles, trying to find that tombstone I was first introduced to as a stoned-out kid on some booze cruise hell ride, where all the fellow stoner kids would pile out the lonely dark old country roads and walk up the hillside into the woods to sit among the dead and use the headstones as seats to rest on while we drank our booze and smoked our weed. We never needed to tell each other ghost stories or try to scare each other; it wasn't like that, we were just simply content to be among the eerie silence of the cemetery and dig on the whole vibe of it all. It was like a drug, like another high in itself, to get in touch with the dead things within our own souls and mix them into the surrounding environment. Even now, as I still drive out here, I still sometimes catch my wandering mind wondering and marveling the early winters chill of insane masses of magic blackbirds making pitch-black blankets over the snow-covered fields, and I ride my brakes in a yield as I drive around the circling country road corners, cutting through the untold age-old stories unread yet already sold to eager minds and what they may find.

The years filled with tears, some from sorrow, others wept in joy, troubling tomorrows of my free bird girl who flew away while giving flocks of blackbirds to her one true lonely boy. I can remember coming down the bend through the valleys of madness, minding my own business of big beauty in bashful bright light white covered in gray skies, the dirty snow melting under dark clouds in her mesmerizing bewildered eyes. I always drove with caution as flocks of crows and ravens surrounded blackbirds and fought them, and somewhere in this lonely back-wood road drive, I unknowingly, subconsciously sought them—the dark warm depression that collected the tears and brought them. My one-of-a-kind irreplaceable love sometimes by my side and other times in my arms. Ever since those days I find myself always returning. For now as the ravages of time keeps going, it is not just the old witches' graves among the familiar graves out here but hers as well; she is gone, no longer living with us in this world as we know, passed on to the beyond. The beyond keeps calling me, and I keep returning. To reminisce? Sure, but to also get in touch with that age-old wisdom of spiritual awareness, a place only the daring and truly enlightened would tread. There is a center inside me that is recharged by the darkness and the places in that darkness that gather the paranormal sensation of the company of watchful eyes from beyond. When the hair on my arms and neck rise up, I know I found those old witch ley lines in Witchwood Forest. I long to see her again and hear her whispering voice. Sometimes to call out the dead, I would have to pick her out of the horde of lost spirits, which was never really hard to do. My love.

Long ago, as a lost boy I used to wander and wonder if they were only some kind of urban legend among the local misfits and outcasts of pagan and wiccans and occult-loving stoners. We, the people of the night, pushed farther into the outskirts of our little Christian and Catholic towns and deeper into the awaiting loving embrace of the shadows that were always waiting there on the edge of the witchwood—a gathering place for us among the twisted old trees. How many years have they seen before any of this was even here? When I say I'm not the only one to gather here, I sincerely say this in reminiscence and recollection of those who gathered among me in the shadows, passing around joints and sharing hits of blotter acid and washing it all down with swallows of cheap wine lovingly passed around from left hand to left hand and down the left hand path.

Up over the hill, past the cemetery and down the descending path into the woods by the dark Devils Creek and the old bridge were the wind whispers through the rustling leaves in the twisted treetops where the ravens nest, occasionally letting the lunar magic of the moonlight through to reveal the watching shadows that linger and follow with those watching eyes of fondness, keeping me company tonight in Witchwood Forest. How long, I ask, must we wait for that realization that the things from our darkest imagination are indeed all real, or do we continue on through another century of denial and fear? The darkness and what's in it comforts me. Even when we were tangled up in each other making love like two stoners do, in the back seat of my then 1970 rally sport split-bumper Camaro, her perfect soft lips on mine were sweeter than all the grass and pills combined.

She was the best drug on earth. Ecstasy and love in the pitch-black night, now just memories.

The winding trail twisted further into the darkness, with the weed-infested dew-dropped spiderwebs and rotting corpses of raccoons and possums, the skeletal remains of some potential necklace, possum skulls, and candles. The sweet smell of weed in the summer night air telling you that you're getting closer to the summer's big crop. The marijuana leaves fan out as the very hand they say reaches out for yours to drag you to hell—that sweet killer weed with the roots from hell. I always loved how the yellow-and-black orb weaving Illinois banana spider would weave its intricate silk zigzag signature within the buds of the plant in late fall, clinging the huge sticky buds tightly as they sway in the autumn wind in unison. Someone will adore smoking that magic in late winter months of madness. Those dusty cobwebbed memories of seasonal depression bring me back full circle in the hot, humid summer night air.

I take sloppy drunken steps down the crooked trail to the creek side to look at the rippling full moon and call the following spirits to come gather a place around and behold divine existence in open awareness of this world and theirs. The thin walls of the spirit world become easier and easier to cross. It's this wall where I can feel them reach out past that bridge and gently brush my arm and whisper my name. I always know when they are near from the sensation I get. The hairs on my arm and neck tell me they are among me, still watching. There was deep sadness of the dead and the deeper sadness still of being discarded, left behind to walk along knee-deep in the itchy overgrown weeds of those lonely twisting country roads. Grasshoppers jump from old wooden fence posts onto my sleeve to catch a short ride and look deep into my eyes as I wander down the left-hand path into the Devils Creek of Witchwood Forest to watch the moon in its rippling surface, all the while knowing perfectly well what lingers beneath the surface of that dark creek's currents. Somewhere there is an undertow rolling around bones of the unfortunate. Rolling around in my head are these terrifying images of a lonely and depressed mind in solitude. The curse of isolation from the smiling enemies in fake plastic smiles. The masks worn by the beast. Not my beast, just theirs. My gods live and let live and don't torture the different. The outcasts, the misfits, the pagans, and the occultists don't need them. We have Witchwood Forest. Fuck everyone else.

I reach into my pocket and pull out my one hitter pipe and smoke more reefer, the devil's harvest, in my hands. The sweet-tasting cannabis soothes it all and puts me back in a calmer touch with the nights surroundings. I can't escape the grasp of this place, as it always seems to keep calling and pulling me back here. It is the time I patiently wait for, where the ancients and the spirits of beyond come to dance with the undead and play in the shadows with lost forgotten dreams. There is a vision of a broken clock on the wall, its pendulum stuck as the clock collects cobwebs, and seasons come and go in lonely despair—timeless and ageless. The echo of a loved one's voice long dead and gone, my name being called by those I have loved and hold dear—the torment of it all is they never say much more than just my name, just the bitter sting of that brief stimulant of longing and missing the ones that are no longer of this world. They sleep now, with my sorrow.

My shoes accumulate the moist remnants of weeds and dew as they collect on my lower pants legs. I shift lonely strides into the darkness downstream along the dark currents of Devils Creek. The weeds and muddy banks hold me a couple feet higher than the black water's surface. The eyes of Witchwood Forest follow me as I take a seat on an ageless moldy tree log, covered in moss and algae as it crumbles slowly over time back into the creek's banks. I pull out my pinch pipe for another sweet pull of the devil's weed and gaze up through the tree line to see the silhouette of the old tombstones on the hill in the clearing as the moon light glows down enough lunar magic for me to my watchful followers drifting among the headstones in their dark shadow figure forms. I remember yesteryears in days of my youth holding séances with fellow pagans Some have seen her in white flowing gowns, some have seen her in the form of ravens. Hundreds of years before they ever dug the first hole to lower down the first soul into this valley, the tall prairie grass was drenched in blood by those town dwellers' ancestors as they murdered the pagan witch. Her glossy eyes pulled in the last bit of that same moonlight as she gasped her last breath here on Witchwood Forest. Her blood smeared on the surrounding weeds and seeped into the cold ground. A hundred years before that, long before these woods were ever called Witchwood, they were considered sacred ground because of the thin wall between our world and the spirit world.

A brave Native American warrior of the wolf clan lost his life to the neighboring raven clan of the same tribe over a beautiful and lovely Native American princess who walked and hunted these forests, so long ago before that the echo of life and love have seeped into the roots of these old woods and stains and haunts them with those residual energies. If you stand in the same place long enough, eventually even the blind lost dead will feel their way to you. Sometimes I occasionally feel their touch, a cold chill that most people pretend is not real. Denial or awareness? I died enough times at the very hands of those that I loved to learn that even angels are sinister and deceiving. As sure as fact that everyone and everything dies with their own private expiration dates, everyone and everything lies, and if they say otherwise, then they are lying. Denial is just a crippling, disabling poison that dulls our natural basic primitive instincts and slowly blinds our eyes, yet people do it because it pays to be blind.

How can you be afraid of the demonic shadow walker stalking each one of your steps further into Witchwood Forest when you can't see or feel its empty heartless soul creeping up on you? It's a painless, stress-free ignorance that only makes you an easier target of those who mean you harm and wish you ill will. I am driven completely mad and insane by forcing myself to keep an open mind, even when my mind itself attempts to retreat in self-preservation to avoid the pain of madness and all the psychotic features that go with it. I will deal with that hellish repetition to reap the rewards of breaking free of insanity's grasp. Waking from a nightmare and coming down from a bad acid trip are just a few of the many ways to explain the rewarding moment of clarity from fighting through the grip of madness. Of course if you keep your mind closed and become a skeptical atheist, then you may escape a lot of deep, puzzling realizations and save yourself the annoying torment of hearing many different voices of many different things from many different places. But I prefer the freedom of tuning into the messages from beyond, if not for my lost love then for any other reason than using all my senses and being more aware.

Something is out there in Witchwood Forest along the old ley lines and old-time black magic. Out here among the moving, watching shadows in the darkness is my escape from the towns in the valleys below who live by cruel, thoughtless lies of illusion. Out here, I can rekindle and retune my inner primitive senses and instinctual nature that society slowly blurs and dulls away until most people grow so numb of it that it becomes an ignored or forgotten unfelt emotion. Society has become such a mess because this very emotion is one of the most very special ones. The importance of gut instinct and sixth sense in my eyes and heart is what always draws me back up to this old cemetery and the dark woods that surround it. I clear my mind from my own constant frustrations bestowed on me by the negative energy of society's fear of the misunderstood, and I replace it with opening my ears to the silence and listening to distant voices from beyond. I have no fear for the paranormal or the spirits who dwell in the places most people avoid.

Society's greedy coldhearted ways and thinking has dragged me by my heels through the mud with their judgmental hatred for people like me who embrace the very things they hate and also make me different from them. All their lies, rumors, and gossip can't hurt me among the dark enchantment of the spirit world, the ghosts, the things that know what most of the living do not. I take another pinch hit of weed and clear my mind and begin tuning in with the night, returning my glossy stoned gaze back up through the path and onto the moonlit cemetery hill looking for the shadow figures among the old weathered headstones. Nothing up there in that cemetery or here with me in these woods frighten me like the persecuting judging of the two-faced smiles given by those "good people" in the city. Even as I watch the shadows around me shift and move, making me aware that the ghosts of Witchwood have started to gather around me, I am nothing more than another animal retuning my primitive instincts and senses, those very senses and instinct most people blind themselves from as they slowly let the illusions of life blur and dull them away until they become numb of them.

Out here in Witchwood Forest, I feel the dread of the outcast slowly fade away with my ghostly ancestor company, those beautiful interesting pagans who danced with the dead to the beat of their own drum among nature's spirits, persecuted and judged for running from the cruel rules and punishing consequences of choosing to follow one's own heart over the constant bullshit brainwashed into our minds from youth and on up. I thank my heathen ancestors for giving their lives to the spirits of the earth and wind and fire and water, all living things that the rest of society arrogantly and foolishly consider lower and unworthy of respect. My heart breaks and I weep those tears of all the cruelty bestowed by the haunting past. Days of burning pagans at the stake and hanging them from the branches of the nearest tree have been replaced with a process of rumor-starting and gossiping to exile people like me and myself. Loneliness is a curse I, too, have also embraced.

The ravens land on the cemetery head stones to catch a reflection of me in their knowing eyes. Along the Devils Creek in the darkness is a sinking feeling in the pit of my stomach that everything has been taken away from me, stripped of an open, fearless awareness and conditioned to look over my shoulder as the things from the shadows come creeping up to embrace the sadness and use it to possess the weary mind of lonely questioning. Sometimes I just want to let them take me somewhere someplace far, far away from here. I am driven by demons into the never-ending dark, calling the echoing void. Shadow figures line the trails, beckoning me to climb back up the trail and bathe in the lunar glow of the watching moon. Some people somewhere told me about the red blotch on the blood moon and how it separates certain people from the others. The expanding void and the doors that go to nowhere. I've been chosen since the drawing down of the moon ceremony marked me for this day. Listening to the spirits whisper in the night was just a small beginning of timeless conversations of deep hidden secrets too intense for most people's simple minds. I am adored and watched by those who can't bear to see me go and those who call for me to join them, torn between that line of two worlds—ours and theirs, the living and the dead.

The ancient history of these woods and the mysterious ley lines fill me with a sense of knowing that most people dread. As I walk out into the clearing among the crumbling weathered headstones, I feel those things beyond most people's understanding accompany me. Walking into the woods along Devils Creek has always been just another thing people dread, questioning eyes held back by fear. I am stained with these secrets of forbidden knowledge. Questions people are too scared to ask, so instead they waste time and money going around what only takes a few steps to go through. I walk through the threshold onto the moonlight's magical age-old essence of illumination. There is no escape. The distant howls of wolves drown out the fading memory of what I left behind, and the reality of here and now is seeping into this enchanting awakening. The crickets chirp, and the owls occasionally chime in as I feel the shadow figures surround me. "You are here," one whispers into my ear as the chill of undead hands upon me pull me into the maze of old collapsing headstones. "You are here with us now" whispered again into my ear. My stoned glossy eyes scan the shadows of the graves in the moonlight leading up to the grave I came here for. I reach into my pocket and find my oxycodone bottle and sprinkle out six of the 7.5s into my hands and wash 'em down all at once with a swig of sweet-tasting Jack Daniels from my pentagram flask—the familiar bittersweet burn that warms my lonely soul and creeps up like hellhounds in the darkness, an adoring loving redeemer for all my pain and suffering. It was all just an annoying illusion. The beauty and magic are what are really real, and I embrace it more than anything else. I finally answer back to the spirits that surround me as the cool night summer breeze blows my long hair in matted tangles into my numb face, "Is she here?" I ask. I want to call her name, but silence is sacred, and my heart can't bear to hear it said out loud. Love echoes through monumental monoliths that most people ignore on their speedy quick way to somewhere unimportant. My love. All I ever wanted among this tough, cruel world of beauty and pain, insanity and letdowns was love. Love was and always has been more important than money or anything material. Perhaps I would be lying to myself if I said love was not what made me believe in magic. After all, is not magic and love in so many ways one in the same? At least if anything, they do and should and always have and will go hand in hand in some dreadful and haunting way that captures the heart and touches it.

They say if you love someone then set them free, but no one realizes that no matter how free love can fly away, it always comes back to haunt you like swarms of chaotic, hectic flying bats, surrounding its thought-consuming obsessive heart ache of what is limited—my time. The race of the last caress and sweetest of kisses before the beautiful sunrise on dawn's painted skies washes it all away in some inner reflection of distant farewells and goodbyes, the bittersweet parting of a dying soul meant only to let go. That stain of sorrow is never set free; it lingers like the smell of her clothes and perfume and the taste of her lips on mine. She is not gone, just sleeping in the night. Somewhere long ago, she was curled up in her soft bed that also smelled of her, her scent in the warm silky sheets and satin pillows that rested her beautiful head—a place I longed to be. That place is forever gone, replaced by the cemetery's cold ground of dew-dropped weeds and forgotten headstones in a lonely graveyard in the midnight moon light. I long to see her ghostly image drift out of the darkness with open arms to claim me and take me with her through that passageway into the beyond.

No one wants to know what happens to lost loves as the ravens come down and behold my presence to catch a glimpse of the last of the rare and true souls while most of the rest of the world become deaf, blind, and dumb. I keep my eyes open for what scares the living hell out of the ugliest and meanest of monsters. An endless love through the ages that can never die. I am already silently dead and drifting to those who know the difference, and yet no one is brave enough to utter the words out loud, not even me. Like some bad acid trip in some hellish nightmare, denial keeps me here, and refusal to fight is my curse. I am dreadfully dead and insane. *No one* should ever know the painful insanity of solitude's captive grip, *few* could ever brave it. No one is there to offer comforting words or a human touch, just me and the things not of this world. Have I died? One can only guess. Do I care? Caring is just fuel to the madness; sooner or later anyone in my condition, in my predicament, will eventually stop caring. Caring hurts; it's easier to let go and give in to the awaiting embrace of the night—the embrace that eagerly and yet patiently awaits like an obedient loyal servant with a promised order given, waiting to take me into the darkness into the arms of the eternal bottomless, endless void of the night.

The sunrise's dawn shuts the door behind me, forever gone. The deceiving laughter of tormenting madness reminds me there is no one to call me back from wandering farther and farther into the darkness looking for the ghost of what she was once, the distant fragile remnants of anything left. The moon slowly creeps across the sky as the search for her among the dancing dead and lost souls surround me, brushing their caressing cold hands across my face and pulling me in every direction. I glance down the cemetery hill back down onto the twisted windy blacktop country roads where the bridge stands over Devils Creek. I long to see her ghostly silhouette and see her reach out to me. I glance down the road over the hills and through the thick forests to see a distant glow of the small town miles away over the tree line and listen to the silence of the night, the gentle chirping of crickets, and realize I am content here standing in this old graveyard in Witchwood Forest, far away from the hateful judging looks of misunderstanding conformed, outstanding citizens of society. I am an outcast, a misfit, a gossiped, rumored, and feared, shunned unwanted shadow walker. I don't belong with them, and I only feel at home here in Witchwood, away from it all. I scan the horizon and up and down the twisted blacktop country roads once more, then I look back up behind me at the Witchwood cemetery alongside the forest and past Devils Creek. I let out a sigh as I feel the Oxycodone start to kick in. Oxycodone and Xanax were my favorite mixtures, a feeling that it would bring of a painless, carefree euphoria, and among this feeling of not giving a fuck were these things from beyond. I am in exile from the cool people and in company with the outcasts like me and myself. Loneliness is a curse I, too, have also embraced.

The ravens land on the cemetery head stones to catch a reflection of me in their knowing eyes. If I am stained and cursed with hatred and shunning for no reasonable reason other than fear and jealousy or for someone's own vindictive self-amusement, then I will not let it destroy me but instead embrace it. Even a misfit among misfits for years, I suffer stranded long enough to have gathered a love for the spirits from beyond, who make the shadows and lonely places not scary at all. I've grown stronger within myself as all the endless countless nights of solitude and those spent running with the same wolves of my nature opened me to something so much more beautiful than mankind's arrogant crowning achievements. Fuck society, fuck the world, fuck all the rules and painted illusions of what we are supposed to believe. I believe in what most people refuse to even consider, that the entities and whispering apparitions that comfort me in my solitude all know. If you take a journey with these words I am giving to you, you can join me and walk beside me through these dark woods, and I will show you things far more beautiful and spiritual than anything that may have you trapped and contained in some bullshit illusion of lies and hatred that force you to have to put on a mask every time you walk out the door. I tell you, you don't have to smile if you don't want to. You don't have to participate in their mundane repetitious small talk, and you don't have to stand there helplessly as you're forced to listen, no matter how much you try to fuzz it all out, their annoying laughter of two-faced gossip that will invade your desperate longing for a piece of mind for peace of mind. Fuck them all.

I hung my head in brokenhearted seclusion and took them long lonely walks into the forest to find that escape so many times. You are now in good company; I want to take you with me when I die, so hold your head high and walk beside me into the darkness. Don't be afraid, I am going to be your spirit guide and set you free among the spirit world where there are still rolling hills of endless trees and creeks and open valleys and fields under the moonlight that mankind hasn't gotten their dirty, filthy destructive hands on yet. When you feel you can take those steps alone and are ready to let go, I will not ask you to stay; possessions and control are just part of the illusion I want no part of. Everyone, it seems, wants to control everyone else, losing sight of their own inner self. I hear it in the tones in people's voices, that fear of lives' natural chaos that can't be controlled, and yet people hypnotize and brainwash themselves.

I remember back when the early first few rides to Witchwood Forest were adventures. We would all take turns climbing up on the top hood of the car, and after any of us felt we had a firm enough grip on the hood of the car, we'd give the others in the car a signal, a hold-on for an authentic, sincere hell ride! Weaving in and out of the curved, winding twisted blacktop country roads that cut through forests and old graveyards. These old stories of decades gone and past in a simpler yet darker time still swell within my heart and bring tears in my eyes, the coldness, loveless, and emptiness of being unwanted by society and embraced by the same other outcasts and misfits. That same feeling that comforts in the cold, wet mornings has always been in these woods and among the headstones of the buried and forgotten.

There is a lonely weed-covered, mistreated, unkempt, and almost-forgotten headstone out there, out here among us. It belongs to her, and it is as almost as distant and forgotten as her long past gone laughter that echoed through the treetops of this forest, a dull numb hollow empty hole in my soul where she once was, illuminating lost happiness from that numb missing part of me, the phantom emotion of smiles and smiling eyes through the cloudy thick haze of pot smoke boxed in the parked car at night with what us stoners would call the dome light instead a "dope light" just barely setting off a soft warm glow of her beautiful face in the haze of the midnight seclusions of a cold dark night. I cried while I watched the huge snowflakes in the car headlights while I tripped on acid, later that winter. While on an acid-trip winter drive out in those same country roads in the middle of a blizzard, how my heart longed for her then, but by then she was already gone, and the winter clothes and warm car heater that helped melt each snowflake on the windshield were just reminders that the same snowflakes were covering her grave in the cold ground of Witchwood cemetery. I knew I had people who loved me waiting for me in a warm cozy home; the warmth of loving laughter that would fill the holiday spirit with joy was somewhere lost out here in those cold snow-covered country roads that led up to her lonely grave. Back at home was the kind of joy and love that would never touch that cold dark place out there on the cemetery hilltops, only cold moonlight and freezing blackbirds that would leave there bird claw imprints on the snow all around her grave.

I remember now all the times she touched me and kissed me. Those very same memories were all that were left. I stumble up the snowdrift with an almost empty fifth of Jack Daniels in my hand, dropping it in the snow as I stumble and trip in the snow-covered ground around her headstone, and there she was, among the frozen moonlight and glow of the soft white snow in a lonely lost graveyard. I fall into the snow tripping on acid and too drunk off whiskey to sob and weep the tears of a fallen angel who will never win its way back into heaven, for she was the key to heaven's gates, and it was decomposing in the ground while the world turned and aged with season after painful season of empty hollow heartache. The tears would freeze, and I would weep fresh, warm tears that would freeze over the frozen ones as the howling winter winds would blow more snow over me and her grave. Those past memories of lonely cold winter nights out there have brought me back time and time again for not to hear her voice, as I would regularly hear her voice from time to time as I dozed off to sleep at night or, in my desperate despair, in hollow solitude. I came out there so many times because she will only appear to me in two places out here, Witchwood Forest and Devils Creek bridge, both so close to the point of her death and the place of her rest. Recalling that cold winter night when she first appeared to me in that snow blizzard like an angel in white, among the moonlit snow-flakes that softly floated around her beautiful image, an apparition of wonder, has brought my mind back to the present point of now, the present point in perfect time out here once again in Witchwood. A dark humid summer night, knowing perfectly well where her tombstone still stood yet unable to approach it, as I wander out here alone, I reached a point where I keep a good distance from her grave for as long as I can. Once I'd finally get close enough to see it, I won't be alone. I know my dazed gaze would wander as well to somewhere where my mind could take us. It would take us to a certain point and place in time where everything was bloomed in a perfect state.

Everyone dies, and we all leave and take a piece of one another when we come and go, but as ageless as all the lonely sunsets that fell on me in my heartbroken despair that has come to wash away forgotten lost memories of those blooming wildflowers on the sides of those country roads, the beauty was always mixed with the ugliness of discarded beer bottles and beer cans that littered the infamous place with decomposing road kill and spray-painted bridges. Something more than just her and my precious history of sacred, irreplaceable memories has happened here. Something bigger than all of us has come and gone in the warmth of a sunny summer afternoon and was frozen in the lonely winter blizzards. I was left here to watch it all change while she was gone and to never return; no matter how long I waited for her, she would never return. Then came the nights of the insane berserker within, the inner pagan who listened to the changing seasons long enough to grow with them and hear them speak to me, and with all the spirits of this sacred place, finally came her voice. Her soft whispering voice at first, then later her sweet face, and soon after, were full-body apparitions of my love. As gentle and still as the eerie silence of the creeping electric storms, the breeze would eventually carry in the distant storms with the whispering voices of many, and among them all was her own gentle voice from beyond, calling, calling out to me, whispering my name, my name carried in the haunted, hallowed winds of the infamous Witchwood Forest, among the tangled twisted trees and mangled thorn vines in the overgrown thickets of dead brush and skeletal remains of sacrificial critters used in the blood rituals of old pagan magic. Spray-painted symbols of the occult and the melted remains of black candles on the old Devils Creek bridge would be a grim reminder that there was always a much darker history and darker side to old Witchwood and its magical aura that felt as if you have stepped backward in time in some lost dimension; perhaps it was the old witching ley lines, perhaps it was the energy of all the occultists' spells, perhaps a bit of both and so much more. She was out here and not just always there by her headstone, like some would like to believe, but everywhere, in the trees, in the wind, in the dark undertow murky currents of Devils Creek.

"What did you throw in that creek?" someone asked me once. The sinister grin of those I knew who have indeed threw shit in that creek, even some of my very own heroin stash, ended up in those murky muddy waters as an attempt by concerned friends who say their cruel deeds of dope stealing was in good intention, as they were worried about my soul and well-being. I often wondered if they just said that and really went somewhere by the Devil Creek's banks and did the damn heroin themselves, but I also wondered what was found in that evil twisted creek that cut through miles and miles of witchwood? Some bloated body found wedged up underneath a clusterfuck of rotting driftwood logs? If so, why was I always the main fucking suspect in every damn hellish sacrificial ceremony that took root out there in the darkness? What in hell has taken place along the old lay lines of Witchwood Forest? Haunting deeds too disturbing to whisper even among the dead and lost souls who wander the haunted Gates of Hell. Those who were not hip to even a shred of its lure of lore and history were doomed to catch a glimpse of the pale-faced ghosts within the forest, caught for just the few precious seconds of time in the passing headlights to make direct eye contact with a damned and lost soul. Lest ye be driven by demons? Then they shall drive you, ride with you, take a place in the back seat, waiting for your careless eyes to drift across the rearview mirror and catch the gaze of the grinning demon with its sickening smile of demise.

Rape this world, rape this earth. We as humans are not here very long compared to the timeless existence of things not of this world and so far beyond our understanding. Those things you have foolishly believed do not exist or maybe you brainwashed yourself out of fear and denial, thinking that it would somehow protect you from those things of the shadows and darkness who care not if you believe in them or not. There is only the first step of knowledge and understanding before anything else. Everything here is all going away. *We* are all going away, and when the day comes when I meet my own demise, I shall be in her embrace once again, not as I remember her but as she now is, transformed into something different. The ever so changing mysterious universe was once shared by those who dwell in the shadows and take slow steps in the dark. The devil does indeed creep up beside me, so many times before, disguised as those who say they love me but only speak in the tongue of the serpent—never happy words of encouragement, never caring words of empathy, never the truest or sincerest words spoken in kind tones from the voices that I do love but instead only words of deception in the form of cruel questions in the arrogant tones of those who wish no good. Those who wish no good on me or around me are puppets on strings on the collapsing stage who hate to amuse those who don't give a fuck. Every step of gravel kicked downhill onto the beer-littered overgrown ditches of those old familiar eerie blacktop roads. Country roads take me home where I belong, in the lowland timber of Witchwood Forest, where she lingers in lost desperation of a tormented end to the thing she longed for most. A life. A life with love and understanding and no prejudgments. An open mind for an open soul let go upon the tiny fragile hourglass-like moths dancing around a broken back porch light on another long-lost forgotten night. Her amazement was my delightful enchantment, and her sincerity was broken behind a hesitant shy demeanor from the lies and betrayal from a cold cruel world. I was just a man caught under the spell of the summer's full moon, but when she was in my presence and I held her attention, I was a god among gods, capable of drawing down the moon and giving her power to see and hear those gods and all in their command—the things that we either take for granted or are too blind or scared to see.

Spirits are usually not of our misunderstanding, but the things far beyond our conception are all intertwined. I will ask you now as you read these words: who did you know who listened to the rustling leaves in the whispering breeze on them old twisted branches and heard what they could see in your eyes, that you yourself were too scared to listen as well? Your fear could push you into the arms of the ones who deafen themselves with the city and its fuzzy feedback of annoying noise, like those laughing in the crowded bars and the downtown corner shops with fearful gossip of the ones who ventured past the gloom and doom and the beaten path into the embrace of the nature's symphony of chirping crickets and croaking frogs. My ears are filled with her loving silence as I tune in to listen for her voice among the whispering winds of the locusts and cicadas. Out here in the sacred bosom of the night, even the jesters and fools could not follow. Like the wolf who tests the winds, smelling the humid warm summer night air, there is something out there just out of reach that needs to be hunted and found. This is what separates the leaders from the followers and puts the true enchantment in every waking dawn.

I never ever stooped to the level of all those simple town folk out there past the trees of Witchwood, up there in that soft city glow beyond the treetop skyline and far from the midnight sounds of nature. I never wanted to live up there with all that noise and those lights. I only wanted to shift change into a tiny bat and flutter away high up on the treetops like a genie finally being released from its bottle. Dreams are fulfilled only in my sleep, as I am an earthbound prisoner in this human form. When the hairs on my arms start to raise, I can feel the magnetic field of those old witch lines and what she used to tell me between pinch hits of good reefer and gulps of cold beer as the bottles sweated in our hands in the warm humid summer night heat, "I heard that strange things happen here in these old ley lines since the time Native Americans lived in these woods." She blew out a hit of weed between another gulp of beer. "That is why so many pagans worship the spirits out here." She grinned. I feel a tear trickle down my cheek, and I wipe it away as the night wind starts to howl. I know she is gone in this form, and these are just memories.

I wipe another tear off my cheek and realize that the beautiful face of a memory has faded into a pale foggy glow of smoke-like mist, and as the cool air chases away the warm humid summer night warmth with a cold chill, I begin to notice the ectoplasm shape shift into what she is now, her true form. The air around her chills me to the bone as the hair on my arms stand up, and I notice my breath in visible exhales of anticipation and excitement, as I once again see my lost love's adoring but empty eyes. Those eyes that once held amazement and enchantment forever changed by knowing the forbidden knowledge guarded by haunting nightmares, the torment of knowing what we, the living, are not supposed to know or at least take great comfort in not knowing. When the night breeze blew through my hair and the rustling leaves hummed and buzzed in distant harmony, my eyes searched within hers the apparition of a longing love. Or as the skeptics would criticize, as an active imagination from the local town looney-bin, the bat-shit crazy mad man that wanders Witchwood Forest calling and listening to the dead to pick out the needle in the haystack—a longing embrace from the ones most people believe are gone forever and can never come back. Her cracked, bent, worn-out picture has sat in my wallet for many years. I call her name, and she smiles and whispers "I am always with you, by your side." The dead girl wanders the overgrown weeds barefoot and is stuck with all the clues and advice, except that is one thing she must never say.

We all change, and not just us lost, angry, confused children stuck in aging human bodies, but also all living and nonliving things as well are all at the mercy of the ravages of time, and so all we are given are clues. For there are things that the mind may not be ready to accept, the humbling, heartbreaking, truth that no one can make you see, but I found out through ageless lonely full moons wandering lost out in the country under those lonely stars is this: the truth is painful and the false security of a made-up world is more comfortable and hard to let go. But she is patient, and she waits, as if she will wait forever till the end of time. The old shells of our former selves, stored in some dark corners of the mind why our new selves we accept with every waking dawn, those dawns that look so phony because something is missing, and as I come out here, she speaks to me in soft whispers of secret knowledge. My denial and my fear are holding me here as I listen to the very words that explain all this away. What a big step it is, to face the questions that may have the scariest and saddest answers. No one likes pain, not physical or emotional, and in my drug-induced psychosis, even mental pain can hurt beyond simple words of explanation, for how do you put madness in words that do not sound crazy? It's like trying to spell out a word for heartache, loneliness, and for wandering these woods at night just to see her one more time. Well, *ouch* doesn't cut it. There simply is no word for that pain, and because of it, that pain is scary. So I run from it, but I cannot run from her, my guardian angel.

Anger and hatred is a poison, yet these fill me to the brim, and these consume my loving heart and confuse my rational thinking. I am soaked in the world's blood and stained by its pain. The very hatred I wanted no part of, yet it had found itself in me, and it was pushed on me to the point of bitter resentment. This bitter resentment blinds me and deafens me, and I have nothing left to say. All I want to do is listen, but not listen to the fuzzy sounds of screams and agony, but within it all, her gentle soft voice of love, compassion, and determination. And so I see this same confusion and pain and bewilderment, and I wonder if I caused it within her. Knowing how bad it hurts within me, I fall to my knees and weep once more, not for a tear that will save my cursed soul and not for a tear that will right my wrongs, but tears for her pain and her confusion. I am not her, I am me, but I hurt inside for her. I ache to smell her and feel her warmth and hold her in my arms, but she is cold and dead, yet she stays by my side telling me things she shouldn't know, telling me things I know she should not know along the old witch lines in the dark Witchwood Forest. I wait for her to tell me the words she can never say and search within my own soul to face the exact thing that she can never say that has me stuck here in Witchwood Forest, where familiar faces show silent emotion of pity. I will never know the truth until I can face it on my own, because the truth is horrid, ugly, and very painful. I share these thoughts and feelings, not looking for a pity party but only understanding. I ask her not for forgiveness but acknowledgment for my self-afflicting guilt—something so hard to say is I'm sorry. If they say fight fire with fire, then the real emotional version would be fight cruelty with cruelty, and the feedback whines in the ears of the young musician, guitar in hand, as the musty garage is filled with pot smoke and dreams. Feedback of yelling at her as she yells at you and back and forth when all either one has to do is simply be silent, back up, and walk away.

There is a devil succubus from hell lurking in these woods, quite a few actually, and although I am vulnerable to their attacks, she is immune. Because she knows how to protect her boundaries, and once upon a time she wasn't stuck her under the starlit moonlight, but she ran free under the warmth of the sun, anywhere she wanted to go. But not me, no, I keep coming back here in Hela's Helheim, guarded by grinning demons and weird things of disturbing torment, looking for her. No one is perfect, yet we are punished for not being so, and anything good and sacred is taken away so we can learn through pain how to pretend to be perfect in an imperfect world. We are punished for a split second of time that spirals out of control for the risk that keeps us young at heart.

I was daring and dashing and charming once until life's unseen invisible time broke my spine and blurred my sight. Vanity is an ugly sin, because it forces us to forget that the true beauty in any person is in the inside, not the frail aging body lost to the cold ground. Yet she stood not as I remembered her but as I knew her, a bright glow in the darkness like a lighthouse on the rocky shore. The ocean of dead lingered about in the shadows of the night, whispering hateful things, jealous angry things, whispering insults and put downs and lies lurking in mocking laughter, creeping in the shadows to steal my loving peace, joy, and contentment and replace it with the same envious hatred and cruel heartless misery that keep them bound to this place. I fear and hate all of them for not seeing the true me, which is none of those things. Perhaps I am naive to think that they don't; after all that is what they want, to steal away the goodness and humanity in all of us in an unworldly battle from beyond the grave, a battle we pretend we don't see, but she sees it because she was drenched in it as the insects picked her clean, and I realize the words she cannot say will free us both and just how selfish it is of me to keep holding on.

The first big step is the scariest one. Angels stand in patient silence while demons laugh and tease, and I'm stuck here alone in the darkness realizing the apparition of her is just longing visions through tears of sorrow. All those times I watched her walk down that lonely empty stretch of blacktop country road alongside Witchwood Forest were all just hallucinations. She is gone and has crossed over, and I sit here alone in the dark with sympathetic angels and bloodthirsty demons. The battle they fight not among the old weathered tombstones of forgotten souls but from within my very own soul and yours. Love is everlasting and beautiful but not always strong enough to win, not always strong enough to survive, and not always strong enough to be defended or remembered. The wild rose vines grow from the spiderwebbed weeds to feel the soft warmth of the glowing sun until the parasite sucks it dry, and it withers and dies among the sun-bleached bones of dead scavenger-picked critters. Magical enchantment and the gloomy demise and being eaten alive by the one you thought who loved you is being devoured by the jaws of that that is stronger. So love can wilt and die, or love can slay and conquer. Either way you cut it, it's a cruel world without any balance or fairness to it. Be ready to defend and stand defiant, or the black mold will creep on you and consume you, and no one will come to wake you from the nightmare. It is what it is as they say, for what can you really do? I ask myself this as I cling to her image in the spirit of hope, knowing there is a point for each of us in which we can't return. Hateful words and verbal abuse shock my mighty spirit from the creeping spell of heartless trances and moonlit dances among the graves, and the dead we shall dance till dawn's dew-dropped grass wets our shoes. I know she is out here. She just walked away; she is watching and waiting for me to realize the one thing I must figure out for myself. A heartbreaking age-old question since the dawn of time: why can't I go back? Why can't I come with? Why can't I follow? Only you can answer this, not me. Our hearts hold only what we place in them, even if it is nothing more than an empty silent room filled with memories sooner or later time will wash away.

There are many different theories on time. Time heals all wounds, or time is nonexistent. Whatever you believe I will share with you my deep inner conflict that brings me out here into the still silent summer's lunatics' moon and the shooting stars and the sounds of the night life of chirping crickets in the pitch-black forest. I am not afraid of the demons and dark spirits, lost spirits, and all the other horrid hideous creatures who go bump in the night. Those things that lurk and watch in the cool summer night shadows creep up the trees and flutter over the treetops. Old, ageless, and ancient things not of this world and far beyond our understanding are those things that most people foolishly refuse are even there. The misty glow of cold smoke dances around me as I feel their eyes and watch the shadows fall and drift. The whispering voices of damned souls and things of ill intent is the cold ectoplasmic mist so close I can inhale and exhale her out.

It is her again, and my despair has been lifted as I realize what I thought were hallucinations were really truly her and not a malevolent trickster from the bowels of Helheim's ancient goddess dwelling of a cold, foggy, dark place, with swamps and dead forests with its permanent guests of ghosts and spirits. Unless you truly have enough balls to look into the hollow soulless eyes of the grinning demon, then you can be my guest and believe it crawled from out of the abyss to swallow your soul like a hungry tiger. But here she is, and with her sweet faint voice distantly whispering to me the darkest most well-guarded secrets of my soul and psychosis-induced mind. Spoken to me in her so-missed voice, I patiently wait for her full manifestation as the air gets cold and my hairs rise on end. I look into her eyes and realize it is just as equally hard for me to accept her and what she can't say that it is for her to keep her shape. I know she will dissipate into the summer night air again soon and I will go back into denial and despair, so as her face slowly comes into view, I speak over her ghostly all-seeing empathy and tell her I love her very much and explain that I cannot ever accept what has happened. She responds in a chilling goose bump-inducing whisper of a poor lost innocent soul who paid the ultimate sacrifice and says, "Where is everyone? Why are you always alone?" I try to ignore her because I know giving any thought to what she just said will bring back the creeping fear of not wanting to leave, not wanting to leave her, but also none of this world, Devils Creek and Witchwood Forest. "Are you leaving?" she adds in a soft ghostly tone. "Are you ready?" Her haunting voice instills more fear in me as I realize that I am scared of what she is saying and do not want to give it any thought. "Will you come with us now?" she whispers in a distant haunting voice. The ectoplasm mist expands, and I begin to see the silhouette of the shape of another apparition appear next to her, and as the best detail can be expected from the apparition's full form, I recognize it's my grampa standing next to her. In his exact voice, same as it always was years and years ago before he left, he says my name and smiles.

I know back in 2001 my love was murdered and her precious loved body dumped and discarded in the littered ditch like a piece of garbage. I remember a lot of it in my shock and grief, but the parts that are fuzzy that I am scared to recall was I was there with her. Witchwood Forest is a place I feel at home and whole and grounded, and as insane as that may sound, as I stand under the summer night sky staring at apparitions of my deceased girlfriend and grampa, the frightening feeling of dread overwhelms me. My mind automatically goes back into safe zone denial mode. This part always scares me, but they are loving and patient. I cannot ask her to tell me what she can't say because it is so important I face this sickening fear and realize the one thing only I can realize and face is my own. If someone, or something, even a familiar loving spirit guide from their plane or even a patient all-seeing and all-knowing angel, was to whisper the words that would almost send me over the edge in panic attacks, then it would just prolong my agony and defeat their purpose as my mind retreated in denial. I've been out here so long and enough to know that the bits and pieces of broken sorrow I am so afraid of recalling will scare me and send me falling to my knees, weeping endless streams of tears. I miss everyone I love so much, and I know they miss me, because these are some of the things she whispers to me when we spend time together out here. Things like "Your mom and dad miss you so much and they think of you every day and they want you to come home" have always, as it still do, sent shivers down my spine. I remember so many times over the past decade of lonely times and existence, walking into my parents' house and screaming for them to hear me but to only find the place empty, but the over-whelming feeling that always brought welling tears to surface was, although the house was empty, I could feel their presence and smell them. All those eerie times I'd walk into that empty house I'd reas-sure myself that they just ran up to the grocery store. Once of many times in the Big city, I would go on dope runs with my sister, and it always felt eerie and haunting with all the devil in the details that just didn't add up. We'd drive through the worst ghettos to get the very same dope she had overdosed on so many times, her favorite, and no one in the hood or the local ghetto gas stations would even look in our direction. Then we would always go to the dangerous side of the riverfront and drive down its old cobblestone streets and abandoned brick building that were windowless rubbles of their former glory, and then down past all the gang graffiti were so many souls who lost their lives to drugs and violence. Then along the knee-high weeds on the hidden dirt roads that ran alongside the mighty Mississippi River under their old bridges, we would park.

I had goose bumps on my arms, for I never see too much of my sister. Her addiction had her over here on this side of the river almost always, and mostly with my equally strange and eerie brother-in-law, they had an "inside secret" aura about them, as if they shared a secret crime too morbid, taboo, and unspeakable to mention to another soul, a weird mysterious crime that they both committed that no one knows about, no one knows but them. When I would go with my sister to these eerie lonely spots along the muddy banks of the river, she would never have a shred of fear, not even a fraction, just a haunting sweet smile that she knew something that I did not know. It was one of the things I adored about her. She had a dark sense of humor and the bravery of a lost, hurt soul who gave up caring so, so long ago. I'd eagerly snort up the heavy dangerous street drugs up my nose to ease the pains of withdrawals, and as the slow high crept up my spine in tingling delight and gently exploded in brain orgasm ecstasy into my confused brain, I would watch her do what I always hated to see her and my brother-in-law do, find a spot in and on her scarred-up mutilated arms of twelve years of shooting up dope in her arms.

Those rides were always eerie as they felt unreal, and I remember taking a careful listening ear to her stories as we went there and back, hanging on every word. I'd listen attentively about the few times she shot up dope so powerful that it would be noon when she got her fix, and it would be late evening, waking up from being slumped over the steering wheel by herself in the ghetto for so long. She would come to and then wipe the drool from her face and start the car and leave. My heart would break because I knew that was the only clue she could tuck into a short story without being in the awkward and uncomfortable position of silence. She and my brother-in-law always kept telling me that they died in a grassy knoll on the side of the river and then just disappeared from not being able to say the words to me she must not ever say. Over time these little clues would send me into a shocking state of awareness and fear, as I would slowly realize that there is something not quite right about this world I was living in. Streets and landmarks would mysteriously change, and nothing ever went wrong like the law of reality's chaos. The cops never followed us or cared; no one did. And so when the overwhelming feeling of frightful dread would shock my blind eyes to strange unexplainable truths that scared me to death, I would always go running out here to Witchwood to confront them in private lonely solitude, circling these haunted woods and their magical ley lines among the tombstones with a heavy aching heart and a scared, confused mind.

I would wander in the midnight summer skies under the mysterious stars that never aged through infinite centuries, never changing, and when the lightning cracked in the summer night heat, in the distance out there by the soft glow of my hometown that shined a dull dim light over the tree tops, I would long to see her silhouette begin her traditional appearance, as she would form in a misty foggy glow and drift down the blacktop country road hillside and into Witchwood cemetery, where her small abused body was so laid to rest under an unkempt tombstone that I would pull the weeds out by hand to see her name. She always first appeared where she was murdered and dumped as her frail tiny frame was so heartlessly discarded into the ditch with the rest of all the road party remnants, and there she lay until a morning jogger discovered us, first her leg sticking out of the morning dew-dropped weeds and then her body twisted into my arms as my head was pressed up to my chest from the weight of my body and the muddy ditch. I remembered the low familiar feeling of dying before, as the flies crawled up and down my arms and on my lips. I remember coming too late with dried-up caked blood in my scalp and my face clotted in my nose as a throbbing piercing pain pounded through my skull, and they told me I lost her, that she was gone. Why did she go so quick, leaving me here to summon her with brokenhearted tears and a longing for her to come fill the hole she took out of my soul when she left me? I would never be the same, and as the seasons changed, so did I, as the pain kept returning me to my past obsessing, fixating on old memories until the future no longer interested me and the present time seemed to even disappear into painful delusional dementia.

Over the years of hanging around my family that acted so strangely different because I have grown so strangely different, each month seemed to grow longer than the last as my will to push forward seemed to give in to the apathy of losing all interest in the things to come. Familiar scenery, the familiar stompin' grounds, and even other familiar faces seemed to grow more strange and unfamiliar to the point of difficult confusing states of painful psychosis, rendering me helpless in accomplishing simple tasks as recognizing these places and faces I've known my whole life. I learned to fuzz out the painful details in my self-induced confinement. The doctors, counselors, and psychiatrists later told me and my family that this was normal in any traumatic event, to block out and suppress painful memories. Eventually I returned to the dreadful scene of the crime that the local occultists have adapted as their own to use the residual energy as a spot to do their ceremony and ritual on Devils Creek Bridge, lining both weathered old concrete spray-painted sides with black candles and discarded Ouija boards.

Alone I made my way up and down those old graveyards and Devils Creek until my energy meshed and gelled with the gloomy, sad energy only a haunted cemetery can resonate. It was only then that she started to manifest and appear to me, and my mind still goes into denial despite I've seen and even talked to her more times than I can remember. It is always convenient for me to go into denial than accept her words and recall that night—a beautiful summer night when we first started going out there. Late, late nights parked on Devils Creek road, filling her tiny car with pot smoke and White Zombie on the speakers, we'd giggle and laugh like children sharing secrets and dreams until that first precious kiss on her soft sweet lips. She was my Valkyrie angel, rescuing me from my lonely unwanted existence of being stranded at my parents, young, restless, and bored. She would always jumpstart my soul with joy when I would hear the crackling of gravel on tire as she pulled up my parents' driveway, and my heart would fill with joy and excitement as I sprinted out to her car and see her cute smiling face through the windshield as her excitement showed as well. I'd jump in her car and the presence of an angel was in my midst.

Our energy would mesh into one like giddy school kids with their first crush, and she would lead the way on another nightly adventure, down all the old long blacktop country roads deep into the late night. Around all the familiar curbs of the local stoner roads we'd make our way to Devils Creek bridge covered in spray-painted rebellion and littered in empty beer cans. We would sit out there and enjoy every precious intimate moment with a happy joy only a young couple in love would know. Everything was so unpredictable and nothing set in stone, just young love in all its whimsical live-by-the-moment glory. Summer nights turned to ice-cold bitter freezing winters out there smoking weed, making out, and listening to the nineties grunge music, until spring blessed the dead emptiness with brilliant beautiful green, almost as beautiful as her precious smile. And soon the humid summer nights came, and we celebrated our one year anniversary. Of course we went and saw so many other places than Witchwood's infamous Devils Creek, but it became a preferred place of admiring tradition as it held so many sacred special moments that only someone who truly loved would understand.

Then came the muggy night in July when we were parked on Devils Creek bridge in the pitch silent night, and we saw the shadows of two figures run across the road. After initial shock and mutual acknowledgment, we both laughed it off as stoner hallucinations. I loved her wicked laugh; it was one of an angry mischievous angel, and as I laughed along, her door was suddenly roughly yanked open, and a dirty unkempt tall guy with red hair and a red beard with BO yanked her out like a monster out of a horror movie. I reached out for her in desperation as she began to scream my name, and then I felt the summer air hit my back as something also yanked open my door, but even though I felt the sweaty, dirty, clammy hands pull me back by my shoulders, I did not care who he was, even if it was Satan himself. My mind only held the attention of my love in danger, and

I fought the dirty, grubby grip of the unknown hands as I crawled across the seat to yank her back out of the red-haired guy's arms. I grabbed her with everything in me and freed her from the dirty hick's grasp only to be hit with something hard by a short deformed guy. This inbred-looking guy must have been the one who was pulling me from behind. I stared him into his sloppy smeared coke bottle glasses just making eye contact before I noticed the crowbar coming down again on my head, and in almost slow motion, I fell to the blacktop country road to stare in heart ache at the image of my angel being assaulted before me as I faded out of consciousness. They must've hit me pretty hard because the details of that nightmarish night that I can never fix has slipped through my numb shaking hands that once held her in them.

As the years went by, the details that escaped me always changed by those who weren't even there and by those who wish they were. Everyone missed her. Everyone or anyone who truly loved her never let go of her memory, company included, and so the horrific nightmare that forever haunts me fades into the darkness out on that bridge, where the morning country jogger found us the next morning. We died in each other's arms, yet she left this world and I stayed here stuck and unable to leave, almost repeating the same day over and over again like a hellish version of groundhog's day. The most hellish unbearable detail is she is gone, and the most fearful, frightening thing of my denial is she visits me here. I think I am starting to figure out not only the secret truths she whispers, but all the other stories from my sister and friends, and that very thing I am terrified of, which scares me to death, is a very hard-to-grasp possibility what I slowly have suspected for quite some time. I will not tell you, my dear readers yet, not yet.

The conspiracy theories leave me an antisocial recluse and drive me insane with denial. But I will do the same as those who still remembered me and loved me enough to not forget or ever give up on me, as they patiently wait with adoring, loving understanding and sweet merciful sympathy. It is this—they wait for me because where I am, I can only free myself, but the prayers and thoughts and fond memories help me realize the one opposite thing that our brains are trained to do—question what we are trained to be a part of and conform to and be punished in lonely cold prisons for questioning rules and reality. Now, those very questions we are taught, trained, and punished to never ever ask or defy or question have all been strangely haunting me to the point of painful madness and lonely depression and a deep fear of the unknown and what is beyond this world. If a lost soul is stuck in purgatory, be happy it is not Hela's very own Helheim, but they are so much alike compared to the Catholics' description of a fire and brimstone hell.

As I write this, I must remind you that the rules of purgatory is a waiting period between heaven and hell and minutes can seem like hours and hours can feel like days, and the stay could only be a month before you can "leave" to Valhalla or heaven, or the stay could last many hundreds and hundreds of years, if not more. My brother-in-law would tell me that his baby daughter and his mom who died both "left." It took such a long time to make sense of his strange choice of words. Passed away? Maybe, but he asked me if I was leaving, and then he told me his daughter and mom left. I know now why I have to stumble in the graveled blacktop country roads with tear-filled eyes looking for the angel that was stolen from me. She was such a shining bright light of love and joy that she got to "leave" immediately, only being granted through her love by the caring, thoughtful angels of her heaven to try to help me escape. I remember the words of my demented tattooist friend with his mischievous giggle, how in my lonely times of depression he always reminded me he would help me "escape." I always thought everyone was crazy. Escape from what? These words only kicked in my paranoid mind into overdrive. My fear stems from my lifelong low self-esteem, that I'm just too much a fuck-up to be granted forgiveness and be set free. The tears that stream down my cheeks are tears of feeling not worthy, but feeling not worthy is fine with me if they let me leave this made-up virtual world and join the company of her and all the others I love.

The everlasting afterlife so many of us have a hard time even acknowledging its possible existence has cradled me here like an understanding patient hammock over the torments of hell that I could easily slip and fall into, but I know now that there are so many worse things that are just barely surviving and barely getting by. There is always some other poor soul who is suffering worse. So patience and compassion among other things are the lessons we all must learn. We will all have to face our faults and addictions and see if they can be forgiven so we can join our waiting loved ones in a place unlike hell or this purgatory state, a place where all your loved ones are waiting with patient adoring smiles and open arms. It's a big step; it's scary facing the unknown, and even more scary leaving something I have grown used to, even if it has driven me mad in hellish repetition. There is no specific name for heaven or Valhalla or hell or Helheim, just as there is no specific name for this purgatory that I spent many years not even having a clue that I was existing here in this strange place, but the good souls who are angels in disguise have all been among me giving those clues, along with other friends and family that are also trapped here.

The name of my hometown is called Highland, and that is the very same name they gave purgatory, an alternate fake highland that could pass for the real one, just only… The locals who live here? Well, that was a clue too because only a few familiar faces out of a strangely peculiar changing array of faces that I have never seen here before have repeatedly offered up good deeds and good advice drenched in clues. For so long I dismissed those clues as some weird mental illness; I just wasn't listening because I wasn't ready. There were so many things about myself I needed to fix or confront or change or uproot. I really picked up some nasty habits from some negative energy, negative thinking, and negative actions. I am so lucky that I've never done anything to send me all the way down.

I've been hearing my dead ancestors' voices lately and sensing their presence around. There is an old saying I never really truly understood till years later. I have always been a late bloomer, but as the old saying goes: "If you want to get to heaven, you got to raise a little hell." It took me years trapped here in my virtual fake hometown hearing so many clues and yet not listening that it took a while to see the plain truth in that quote. If you want to be worthy of being in company of mercy and love by wise and caring angels who care, you must expose your wrongs instead of hiding them. You must face your bad habits and selfish and inconsiderate ways and let them be judged so you may understand how to lose all these bad things picked up along the way from bad living with bad choices. Yes, I am a little bit scared, and I don't know who to trust here in my hometown, but I am happy to share with you that my father recently reached out to me and is going to help me "escape" this place and "leave." I have already died. I accept now that I am dead, and soon this nightmare will release me into a beautiful dream where everyone takes care of everyone and the whole cruel hard world of dog-eat-dog "in it only for themselves" attitude will be left behind. The images of this place are almost quite right but not as exactly how I remembered. All these make sense; if a world is created for you based on your memory of it and perhaps a few others, they are not going to get everything, right? Because Witchwood Forest was her door and gateway. Why? That will probably remain a mystery, other than the fact that it was the place I last saw her, a place that was both special to us, and a place sacred in our memories. Some things can only be guessed instead of a one confident explanation, so why Witchwood and Devils Creek is one's only guess, but all this will return to what it was, a memory in my mind as I leave it all behind for bigger and better things.

We are complex animals, the human being, but with all our pros and cons and snags and imperfections. I like to think the house of the father holds a father with a great sense of humor, a loving being, a forgiving being, and I also take pride in saying besides a few lessons learned from a few random verbal abuse and blind eyes to sensitive feelings, that in the whole grand scheme of things I definitely earned my wings. Besides a few random fistfights, I have never seriously harmed anyone or killed anyone and have always been fun and open-minded, passive, and forgiving. We as humans are far from perfect, so if you start doing the math and start looking around and realizing that a lot of shit just is not adding up, glitches in the matrix or what I like to call god-winks, then perhaps you're here in your own purgatory, with whatever name they call it, and it is filled with those kindred loving souls who want to help you "escape" and those hateful, vindictive souls who want to keep you here as long as they can. The not-so-good ones will come disguised sometimes as people you knew when you were alive and as people who want to help but will not.

The first step before you face those demons and face your flaws and imperfections and right your wrongs is this: make sure you're in purgatory first and not still alive because you will be able to tell. People will say and do things that they normally wouldn't say or do when you were alive. The real kicker is, when we all die, most of the time, or some of the time, we didn't even know we did. We just wake up every day dead, dead, dead, dead and don't even realize it. Like a hellish version of groundhogs day and no one is allowed to flat out tell you. The trick is, you have to notice yourself all the weird things that just are not right, all the strange things that you just can't put your finger on, all the odd and peculiar things that you sense deep down within just are not right, because your body's natural instinct will not lie to you, that feeling in the pit of your stomach, that fluttery dance.

An morbid old stoner friend once showed me, and since I lack the basic barbaric skills that are wired in most dudes, I felt sad after he showed me. A country road cruise on a hot and humid summer night drinking beers and smoking weed when my crazy long-haired pal pulls out his handgun and starts shooting shit, simple normal behavior out in the country, then we slowly pulled up to the reflecting glow of a lone coyote standing fearless on the side of the road caught in the headlights. My pal said, "Watch this," and he pointed the gun at the coyote, which instantly put its ears down and tucked its tail between its legs and started hopping on one foot to the next which at that moment my twisted country-boy friend said, "You see how it's doing that little dance? It knows it's coming," and then of course I remember watching the critter be spared as my friend decided to not waste a bullet on the pitiful creature. The lesson learned was a tough one because of the vulgar display of power used to make his point. Every living thing right down to the cockroach who frantically dashes around for its dear life than take the alternative of being smashed—all have that natural instinct when impending doom is near. The longer you ignore that, the greater your danger becomes until death comes ripping you off the face of the earth. That should scare you a great deal because not only does it show that the natural instinct of doom comes creeping to meet your demise, but it also shows the scariest of mysteries that no one really wants to find out. What happens when you die? No one wants to die. And so when the darkest hour descends its sinister shadow on you, and the fear comes, we are trained in the ancient old ways to face death with courage and bravery, but what if it took you when you least expected? Death's bony skeletal hand just pulled your fucking card—something that I often battled and dealt with with confusion and bewilderment. The missing pieces of the things I am scared to remember and the shocking sobering realization that none of this is paranoia? None of this is a delusion? But it is, it's all paranoid self-induced psychosis that I obsessed about and thought about too much until I fixated on it and believed it to be true.

As soon as I doubt it, I glance at the fading apparitions of my loved ones. My lack of faith and willingness to believe has weakened them, and as she slowly fades into the tombstones of the graveyard, I see the disappointment in her forever changed eyes and a painful sorrow creeping over her face. It is sad but true, but my hands are tied as I am stuck between a headstone and a hard place. The painful condition of going mad left me in this grieving despair. Damned if you do, damned if you don't, believe it and go insane while I must train myself to never repeat this delusion, this made-up worlds, and the gods damn the killing floor...for then comes the bad trips of panic and anxiety, and she never would stand for it to see me like that.

Just over the ridge up high under the pale full moon, the lunar glow would light up the old headstones, and up there was the edge of the tree line of Witchwood Forest, an overgrown brush of twisted thorn vines and thick parasitic poison oak vines that clung to the old twisted oaks like the dead reaching from the graves. "What did you throw out there in Devils Creek?" a distant voice echoed through the tall rustling treetops that looked like millions of skeleton hands of the damned reaching up from the hellish pits of the dark abyss. Up there in those rustling treetops came with it an early cold autumn wind ready to blow every rattling leaf too weak to hold on, away into the haunted woods and into the pitch-black darkness. Although those dead leaves blown in the breeze were living organisms, they never lived like me or you or her back down there in the lonely darkness watching, waiting, hoping, as huge woodland spiders creep through the dead leaves as if to lead the way for all the much more ugly, sinister things that creep and crawl up those old fucking trees. Yeah, I guess I'm a weak, pathetic lovesick bitch who can't get over losing her and am not strong enough to "leave." I guess I'm weak and pitiful because I can't let go—the very evidence of these still strong emotions as I take each step farther back down into the dark Witchwood, where the old ley lines lay, where the trail meets the muddy banks of Devils Creek to stare into the wavering full moon in its deceptive beckoning surface.

I walked back down here to beat myself up because if I can't get a fucking grip on my lunatic mind. The forest will take me, and I will sleep along the dangerous yet beautiful currents of the Devils Creek. Only purgatory would ever show the morbid hellish contents of the murky creek bottom, fished out by men who fear and hunt monsters, and fallen angels watch from across those deadly rapids on the other side of the banks to let me know if I'm not brave enough to see what this really is, then they will send the hideous things of nightmares to take my soul—a challenge and a choice. And then there as I gaze at the moon rippling in its dark murky waters, I hear a whispering voice in my ear, "Make your choice, follow the signs," as if it came echoing back from some long-lost suppressed memory on some old turntable of a Halloween record. "Did you make your choice?" and the shadow figures weave in and out of the tree lines following me as I walk along the infamous Devils Creek waters. Those fools in their shiny fancy toys like babies showing off their security blankets, numbing themselves to the reality that it all can be taken away in a blink of an eye, always looking at the wrong times in the wrong hours and even perhaps the wrong planes and dimensions where only certain things inhuman or dead can cross over and latch on like parasitic bat wings. This world's stupid ignorance and false assumptions has forced me to retreat far enough into these woods for her to not see me like this, some frightened soul trapped in this earthly prison of a walking corpse. It is a heavy load, a real heavy load to weigh on a tired, weary soul who has run out of borrowed time and borrowed options.

The choice is now. Do I fall into a psychosis state of delusion and go mad rotting in purgatory and calling out to her from beyond to see me in this condition, a pathetic tattered, battered rag doll that has almost reached the point of being discarded? Upon that sobering realization, I look over my shoulder as I sense her behind me out there under the open night stars in the pale moonlight searching and waiting for me to call out to her. Circling the empty graveyard just as I have done through many seasons in sorrow, and what of the years before? Back when I did not know her and was free of this attachment? If you step up on the escalator with me, you can blow the baby cherub angel air kisses as we drift up into the clouds. But a younger man more in tune with all senses and less concerned of the constant chatter of endless lost souls speaking to me in insults and questions, put downs, and pleas of help, pleas of acknowledgment, just for me to answer back, "I hear you," so they can feel once again something that once was so long ago and no longer is. I am an ancient soul and a bound shape-shifter forced to seek out the creepy dark places that people fear to tread, if not for her then for the freedom to answer without scaring or disgusting people with all their blind brainwashed taboo insecurities, never realizing they traveled through point A to point B, birth to death.

Being blind and deaf to the world because just like the frightened child who covers his eyes through the fairgrounds fun house does not make the things that frighten you the most go away. Denial and closed eyes and deaf ears might protect you just a bit, but it doesn't change the fact that those predators of the dark in their league with the devil have not crept up on you with their private legions waiting to do their bidding, I died over and over that I can walk among the hideous monsters in the dark without them daring to raise their eyes to mine. The fighting angel salvaged from the belly of the beast in the deepest abyss of hell and brought into the gates of heaven is knighted and forgiven and given a shield and sword much in a small way like the frightened Christians he was chosen to fight for and protect. And once anointed by the creation of all, he was granted permission to walk among these very predators that tormented him. It truly all is just another story out of another book, right? How many books are there? How many goddamn religions? And what time traveler through wormholes has come to see this spinning rock in outer space? Blessing the descending mountaintops with bee-infested wildfires? And of the flatlands down in the hollow and empty silent haunted forests are those muddy holes dug out by nocturnal hiders and creepers of the night filled with tangled spiderwebs filled with carcasses tightly wrapped in silk. Bats flutter overhead as the dark spirits drift from treetop to treetop in admiration and respect of a lost king. It was a delusion, and an arrogant one at that. I'm nothing more than a earthbound captive, trapped down here after living for lengths of time incomprehensible to the logic-seeking scientists today, they arrogantly obsess over the one thing that makes the magical uncertainty real—the sacred rule of thumb of it all, the philosophy 101: anything is possible.

Time stands still, it never moves forward or backward; it is simply the same matter that holds water and electricity and heavy objects can fly through it. The serpent with wings and the disc both fly completely different high above in the cluster of star nurseries and inhabitable planets. Those blinking lights up there are nothing but overlooked stars that the dark shadow walkers along the creek side wander and walk, watching, making sure you are always in there sight and never too far away to make a break for it in the pitch-black woods down here on planet earth. They're a wonderous miracle and enchanting chaotic living cluster of everything alive and dead under those star clusters, the flying serpent moving very slowly in one continuous line miles above these dirty murky waters and the disc bouncing around fast and erratic, chaotic and unpredictable. The water's reflection rippling in the moonlight as the lights above light eyes in the moon's image below.

There is this deep tugging amid all this wonder within my heart. I know she is still patiently waiting, and my love for her will not keep her there. The sinking feeling of depression that has numbed me and slowed me to an almost near sloth-like state is the result of heavy heart, and so I begin the dark walk back out of the woods with the hair standing on the back of my neck. As I turn my back to those dreadful murky undertows, I can even hear all the happy smiling beautiful women pretending to be interested in me so they can milk info from me and pass it around to their rich gossiping douchebag boyfriends. "Where do you fish at?" they always ask, like it's some guarded secret, in which I always respond, "Devils Creek," and as those words stir in my mind, the hairs on my neck and arm rise at the thought of what actually may be drifting in those muddy waters. After all, why would they be so interested if the only things in there were oil spills and beer bottles? I often wonder if those more smarter and heartless types were stalking me again on their phone apps and global navigations.

I look up and see the end of the tunnel empty out into the clearing of our old familiar Witchwood Forest. I know she's out there in the lunar magic of the harvest moon, maybe not in apparition form, but we filter through all the whispering calling souls until we recognize our own. We always find each other, but this time it is time for a long goodbye, and then since there is nothing to hold or kiss, I will choke back tears as I shuffle through the tall grass and muddy embankment out to my car. I sit on her headstone, the very same one I slept beside so many times, the very one I passed out in the snow drifts with no feeling of my frozen fingers or face. Years ago, as I walked under the lunar pull of the magic glow of the moon, I felt alive with the shadows, eternal and ageless; now, when I'm in my solitude back in town sitting in the dark in lonely seclusion, the moon that dimly, faintly hovers behind dark drawn curtains don't beckon me through the drapes as it once did, even when I pull the curtains aside to gaze up at the hovering moon in the midnight skies. The longing and beckoning that used to call me to walk under its glow has faded away and disappeared, and I know those feelings all left when she went away. They say you don't know what you got till it's gone, but I beg to differ. I always knew what I had, I just never expected to lose her. And so I find myself out here time and time again, just to see her again. Only in her haunting hungry eyes from far beyond the cold grave am I seen as the caring human underneath all the long hair and tattoos; the drawing down of the pale moon upon her ectoplasmic mist of a reflection of what once was would send the same people who fear me running, with the chills of the all-seeing dead creeping up their fleeing spines. I stand defiantly among the dead like the surrounding weathered forgotten tombstones in the howling wind, the overgrown weeds that tower overhead making the past almost impossible to find even for the bravest of seekers and loneliest of lost souls.

Any person who has not a sincere heart in the moon's scrying reflection on the rippling sinister surface of Devils Creek and its dark murky undertow shall always hold fear in their heart, a cautious step beside mine, always just slightly behind what they fear, the poor lost me who walked among the dead for so long I've become dead myself, and the bravest men shall shiver in dreadful fear. Was it some strange power that thickened my blood and paralyzed women under my despairing magnetic spell, captivating and invading? Not any precious soul shall do, none like hers. Would I return out here among the unholy witching hour time and time again to march to the beat of my own drum? Not at all, but if only that very beating and drumming of my pounding heart could and would call her to me. The haunting question that repeatedly whispers in my ear is not could or would but should. The answer stirs not in a cold heart but a dead one, a broken one, a lonely one that whispers sweet dead roses wilting and withering in my empty hands, the lonely falling petals from the last stand of a dead man's hand, whispering sweet echoing pain, reminding me all the painful lessons of a dark cold cruel world that deserving has not a thing to do with it. Where she is and where I am going holds no material thing, not even dead withering dry petals from black roses.

These lonely steps in desperate despair—I have always been forced to walk in solitude. How many cautionary warnings and paranoid advice fell on deaf ears spoken from the scared mouths of madness? I knew madness like the back of my hand; I knew madness like few fear to pay small thought, the creeping dreadful madness and sadness and heartbreaking sorrow that it rides on. Death comes ripping from the darkness with a quickness on the galloping bones of the pale ghost horse of doom and gloom, and I know I shall see her soon. I am unworthy of any worldly love and unfit for human consumption, like the black mold and mildewed moss that lines the rotting logs along Devils Creek's muddy banks, to bloom the poisonous toadstools and magic mushrooms out of the moist decomposing dead rot of the moonlight glow. I cast a wary eyes, a foggy, glossy hazy daze, into the dark tree lines on the opposite bank across Devils Creek's waters and see those malevolent dark spirits watch from the shadows they lurk within. They watch from a safe distance, yet they fearlessly keep up with my pace always watching, whispering, listening. The cursed earth we walk, the unseen, the unsaid, the unclean, and the undead, the forgotten, the lost, and the friends of the darkness who play the same games with the devil as he always pays his attention with the adoring company of his leagues of the damned, and even on special random and rare occasions, old Beelzebub himself will appear in any form, but the smile, the voice, and the eyes are always unmistakably always the same.

Other times, I can simply feel Lucifer's eyes in the darkness watching with patient, attentive admiration, the haunting possession of the possessed, the "them" and the "they" of an eternal kiss of death which comes ripping out of the dark night around the unholy witching hour of 3:00 a.m., and stories of the cursed, the haunted, the undead in all its mysterious supernatural forms. Even the murky menacing depths of Devils Creek will be looked at in a disturbingly closer observation under pale moonlight pagan magic and the evil soulless actions of the satanic cults who all perform their dark ceremonies on this old maze of blacktopped country roads nestled within forbidden overlooked pieces of land in avoided territory surrounded in suspicion and tales and lore of legendary paranormal phenomenon. The blackest crow that has ever crowed the darkest hour from a tiny beating heart as cold as the tiny pebbles and stones in the muddy banks of that old creek, I stake my dying love for the searching of a lost soul that was brighter than the summer sun, the warmth on her hair, and the smell of her clothes with the scent of spring's new hope of new life.

Better days ahead all washed away by a unforgiving cold storm. The blanket of dark thunderclouds pushed in a cold front; the cold wet winds tangled her hair and blew off her scarf into the wretched grim hands of the cold winds and into the rustling twisted dead leaves of the hissing whispering limbs and branches of the haunted Witchwood Forest, each twisted branch clinging and tearing her scarf as it blew farther into the dark woods. The cold rain under the dark skies drenched her dress, her perfect breasts and nipples showing through the wet dress as it clung to her tight sexy body, her arms reached out as the wind seemed to rip her out of his arms and into the waiting dark embrace of Witchwood Forest. Was it a nightmare? Surely it was, for the darkest unspeakable things came striking out of the forests shadows wrapping their shadow figure clinging clutches around her as she was dragged into those dark deep sticks of Witchwood and Devils Creek as if it was a path to hell itself. Surely a nightmare, a taunting torment of tortured thoughts intertwined with a troubled heart. I never lost her in this way but through those dreaded nightmares and disturbing thoughts of creeping woe and despair. The sunshine of my love ripped out of my arms by the cold dark storms of life, deep into the unreturnable pitch-black eternal void of emptiness. Somewhere deep into that forest are the legions of hideous malevolent creatures and things that should never be mentioned out loud, all in league with the tangled web of Satan's black magic and the pagan rituals of those who danced on their graves and called on them out there. Now it was again my turn once more to walk among the things so feared in the imaginations of most people that avoid this very place with the denial of its existence, yet I walk out here alone for the both of us, for her, for me.

If she appears to me, my broken soul and stolen heart can be temporary mended and found. If she does not appear to me or speak to me, then I seek some type of morbid solitary clarity in the midst of secluded madness that comes with the isolation and the eerie sensation of dreadfully haunted places such as Witchwood. It is a dark tale of "a tale that wasn't right," which really is just a tale that is unfinished to those of you that are true enlightened and awakened, who dare venture with me into these haunted dark hallowed grounds decorated in spiderwebbed weathered tombstones and towering overgrown weeds. I take out the time now to ask you, my fellow enlightened soul, to put on a brave face as you tread further into these woods with me. There is something I want to share with you; whenever she appears to me, it keeps me coming back over and over. Do you understand what I am telling you? If not, just stay faithfully close to my side as I take you with me to meet her for the first time as I did, and then once you see and feel what she does to me, I will not ever have to explain it to any of my true loyal readers, my own legions of enlightened free spirits. We are all a part of a clan now. The minute you followed me into the void, we became family. Any of your lost brave steps into the fading black hole I leave in my wake. The wake of worlds that surround us has made you part of the family of free-spirited and enlightened.

Oh, faithful follower; oh, adoring reader; oh, sympathetic fellow lost soul, wanderlust with me and I shall tell you her sweet whispers behind anxiously waiting huge trees, her delicate hands filled with wildflowers, and a beating heart of excitement and fear as her soft angelic voice whispers the words into my full captivated attention. She always held me there in full attention, hanging on every word. She steps in closer as I give in to the alluring attraction that equally pulls me into her warm private personal space, the small bundle of freshly picked wildflowers drop from her soft pale angel hands into the dead muddy fall leaves of autumn's forest floor, the blackbirds perched in the surrounding twisted limbs all around. We draw in closer to each other as her soft lips exhale warm breath on my ear and her warm cheek brushes beside mine. My heart pounds as she whispers the words into my ear, "You don't have to be blood to be family." So she once told me, in her warm beautiful living state that she no longer is. "Oh ye of little faith" echoed into the darkness from the eternal ageless souls of yester years, lost forgotten words and actions all now just a faint residual energy. It was a heartbreaking memory, and there was an overwhelming feeling of being at the mercy of painful, uncontrollable feelings spawned by an original pure innocent love set free in the beautiful fall weather of red, yellow, and orange leaves and rotting jack-o'-lanterns. The old punk stoner rebel in knee-high combat boots and trench coats and the league of the enlightened, the free spirit, sang along with the misfits how we all remembered Halloween. We all know no shame, no regrets, and all share a burning, raging passion from what lies beneath long-lost forgotten loves and what lies behind the lonely dark shadows. We have questions that pain and facing it alone can't always answer. Who will walk or run away like all those frightened souls in denial, for if you cannot come with me and let me sweep the dust away from your own grave, then perhaps these memoirs of heartache and transcripts of lonely solitude will never enlighten you, but instead you will be the one who will close your eyes while walking into the haunted house. Lost time, more lost time—the empty dusty rooms of the abandoned houses of our loved ones once held memories of laughter and happiness are now just silent. Eerie silence. The eerie silence of no silence, for every time I tried my best to untune her out, her whispering voice, just like so many others before, I wait for my ears to take a step through another realm and truly hear. I hear the painful reminder that we both equally long for each other and still ache to be in one another's arms. And as the ravens and crows caw in the haunted treetops, I think of this, and I think of her, as my steps shuffle through the weedy spider-infested dead fall leaves on the forest floor.

Autumn's cold chill and the walls of our world and the spirit world grow thinner and thinner, enough for the spirits to crossover. Hugging a ghost? Kissing the cold mist may sound insane to all those who have lost touch with our basic primitive human instincts, our animal nature. I beg to differ; if not for the complete seeming waste of time of the close-minded shallow thinkers and the local regular beer drinkers, are those like me and you, who would rather venture alone into the haunting darkness to face our own demons. To hold her, to see her, to hear her, I would fight the demons of hell and face more than my own demons and every monstrous brutal dark things of the spirit. We all know that when that time comes, most people, no matter how brave, will run, run from something that cannot be outrun. This is a grim reminder of impending doom and gloom's age-old design of a tortured soul's ultimate demise. No escape, no way out, no fixing or curing fate. I've never been able to barter or bargain with death's option of bittersweet borrowed time without talking to the devil and the many forms he takes. Yet out here among the eerie silence of rustling treetops and whispering dead and the occasional raven's caw, I tread further down into Witchwood cemetery, where her tombstone stands out as a new addition in a unkempt, forgotten place. I wait and I wander, listening for her faint whisper say my name, "Oh, Daniel, I am here, my love," and my name repeats in a teasing, taunting way that would send most people fleeing with raised arm hair and goosebumps, but those people are blind, deaf, and dumb. I know what she shares in her new space and time, and as I said before, I will face the most fearful and dreaded monsters of the abyss to look into her eyes once more. I wait for her to appear, not as I once knew her but as she is now, so many times before, before I lost her out here in Witchwood Forest. Since she was torn from my life, I never really could ever let go or move on, especially after she appeared to me once, then twice, then numerous times, a former version of herself as we all know today in this world as a ghost, but anyone who has really seen and talked to a ghost can all agree they don't wear sheets with holes cut out of their bloody eyes, streaming down like morbid teardrops of a lost soul condemned to never see. No, my love has eyes, and she can see me just fine. It is I who cannot see her entirely and definitely not ever the way she once was.

"Daniel, oh, Daniel, my love." I hear her as I step closer to her grave and pull the weeds away from the headstone as a crow's Caw echoes over my shoulder, filling the eerie silent ears of the dead. I remember falling asleep in the snow drifts next to her grave with an empty bottle of Jack Daniels to keep me company. Eventually my face, fingers, and toes grew as numb as my heart and soul, even the tears that would trickle an inch down my ice-cold cheek would freeze to ice, just to have the next tears freeze over them. It was all worth it to hear her again, to see her foggy faint image in the snow, flurries of ice-cold Midwest winters snow drifts, to hear her speak the word I so long to hear—my name. If she couldn't appear to me, then I would be fine with the grim and gloomy option of freezing to death and joining her from the beyond the grave, Oh sweet death, one last caress—I have longed to follow and join, only to endure a curse of being too weird to live and too rare to die. Sure, I'm dying, I'm just not dying like she or the rest of the world is. I'm dying a slow painful ancient and ageless miserable way, the first step through the doorway into insanity, however that door is far behind many moons and mad seasons ago. The only time I ever even felt a shred of sanity in my entire lifetime was through a few handfuls of lost loves that were meaningful in the beginning but horrid in the end, so ultimately the "piece of" peace of mind or perhaps better said a quiet happy silence within was always abruptly put to a hectic, chaotic, painful end. Heartache, loss of love, loss of hope, loss of interest are all swirling into a sinking cesspool of painful madness and a generous dose of general confusion that has left me out here wandering these tombstones and old woods along the Devils Creek for what seems like centuries.

The antagonizing lack of comprehension of time where minutes seem like hours and drag on. Sweet death stalks in the foggy shadows asking if I want mercy from this pain, but the old reaper asks in a gentle way, always keeping his distance in a loving, admirable way. If I was to even acknowledge his existing presence, he kindly steps back into the shadows and therefore I pretend to not see him, just admiring him out of the corner of my eyes like you would a black widow making its web in the corner. Live and let live until the darkness comes to claim me once more. I wish I was somewhere with her, the gentle smile of a true lost soul, perhaps an angel who was taken away by the wrong side, perhaps a painful transition that I wish I could've prevented.

How did she go, you may ask? We were lost together on them old humid dark back country roads on some grand scheme of trying to escape the pain and finding the true happiness that we all as humans seek and hope to find. Some escape from the distractions of all the heartless bastards and bitches that reared their ugly heads toward our direction with their ugly jealousy and their own unconfronted insecurities of the painful madness within us all. She was my escape, and I must confess, for being a lost tortured soul condemned to utter confusion, she was my inner silence and peaceful frame of mind. Her angelic smiles dulled the pain and washed away all the confusion in hot-boxed cars filled with the sweet and sour smell and taste of sweet sativa and the refreshing taste of ice-cold beers. We were young, proud, and free, and she helped deliver the goods every time if you know what I mean. The sweet, merciful love of the mushroom psychedelics ate away the hatred and replaced it with sweet, kind happiness and joy like some cool summer shower on a lazy lost forgotten summer highway. The madness can indeed set us free, if any of you can dare take on the pain that comes with it. My madness started in some painful tiny crack in the bottom of my heart and spiderwebbed from there into total heart-wrenching sorrow that only a fallen angel cast from heaven would understand.

The poor misfortunes and consequences resulted from making choices that angels are supposed to be perfect to make. The old saying "Nobody's perfect" pertains only to humans and not the divine guardians of the creator, yet when you're tricked into doing something insanely different or weird, then there sadly is hardly any mercy or forgiveness, which has always deeply saddened and confused me. If God is so merciful and loving, then in the word of Jesus himself, "Why have you forsaken me?" Because in order to be set free in any spiritual sense, first you must know pain. Pain is a lesson learner right from the start. Burn your hand on the cast iron and never do it again. Do it once, shame on me; do it twice, shame on you; do it three times, and well, you know the rest.

The unholy Trinity—the tritone calling once forbidden in all churches from ancient times when temptation could cost you your life. Any fool who gives into the devilish dark side never returns but rarely and seldom. Love becomes the lack of sun in a dark, dreary overcast of bat-infested thunderstorms and spider-infested graveyards. The gloomy doom of the cursed painful lost souls who can only know the hurt of leaving a lost love behind and the haunting dull numbness that echoes the words that come with it—"Take me with you when you die." Unfortunately the curse of being in this mortal body is simple; no one can take anyone with them in organic form. Crossing over is something we all must face alone.

I wish and dream of happier times when it was just her and I out there on them old back-wood country roads. The time of her departure almost was mine as well, and although I lived to tell this tale, a part of my inner workings was forever removed without a second's warning or any moment's notice to prepare or even fathom the pain

I would forever carry and endure on this earth. Living near the bigger cities always had its pros and cons as with anything else, and the cons are sometimes the cruel, heartless bastards that can only think of themselves in their obsession of being the victim with bad luck placing them on a downward spiral, spinning out of control. These miscreants of society in their predatory thinking, who are always on the hunt for their own selfish needs, have missed the biggest lessons from finding joy in the simple things in life. These are the living, breathing monsters in human form that do a lot more than just go bump in the night, and as it were, so sadly with great misfortune that those monsters found me and my love that dreadful night. A place to stop in the dark night and drink a few beers and smoke a little weed was a local party spot for all kinds, and in my small town everyone knew everybody in some form or way or another. She was as radiant as any midnight love awoken in soft-spoken dreams on starlit skies, a full moon wish upon shooting stars and falling meteors into this tough old world's atmosphere and down here in the mucky murk of sin with the rest of us. Her smile, her laughter, her presence made almost everyone around her take notice. With White Zombie playing loudly over the speakers "More Human than Human," we passed around our reefer bowls and shared stories of Egyptian queens and kings under the sun god's gate to the tree of life, then came the headlights, slowly creeping up the spray-painted graffiti bridge with its littered ditches of empty whiskey pints and beer bottles. "I wonder who this is?" she said with amused curiosity, both expecting to recognize the vehicle or those within it.

As we both watched the two get out of the busted-up pickup, we both realized that dreaded feeling that creeps up on ones' own self when human instinct whispers in your ear to be on guard because something does not feel right. "Who are they, honey?" she asked, and before I could reply, her door yanked open to blow in the cool night air, which caused me to ask, "Who are you guys?" But before I could finish the sentence, I watched the shadow figure in the dark yank her out of the car like a thief in the night, her startled screams filling my bewildered ears and shocked heart as I felt my back give in to the gravity of my own door being yanked open and being yanked out into the dark night. The last thing in my eyes was the weed smoke-filled car dome light flickering with the movement of the sudden jolt of unprepared horror that fell upon us. We both have been unknowingly yanked into the eternal void's shadowy doorway into the abyss of the unknown, the bottomless abyss that took her away and with her all that was left of my shattered, dazed, and confused mind of trust and secure faith of love.

The broken mirror glued back together never quite shows a true reflection of what anyone who experienced a traumatic event knows. That something that was once there within is now missing, and no matter how long or far you stare into the darkness of pain within one's own eyes, from any perspective, romanticizing, hoping, or wishful thinking just cannot reshape or reform the once true happy soul in its former glory. They say what does not kill you only makes you stronger, but it's relighting the flame and rekindling the fire that is the most important fire. When I wander out here in the dark, it is like reaching into the cold dew-drenched wet coals of that fire and finding some way to relight that old burned-out fire that dark forgotten loneliness had long since caressed and dimmed each last dying ember into the cold wet ground. My love that was so warm and full of light is now cold, dead, and in the wet muddy moist charcoals of rotted wood. My tears only saturate the heart-wrenching memories even more, and who is going to hand me any lighter or match out there beyond the glow over the tree lines into the hustle and bustle of the city with everyone on their own selfish agendas and greedy fixes of dope, money, and lust? Out here in the sounds of solitude and in the heart of my madness, past all the watching eyes of the dead and the whispering voices of those lost is a distant evil chuckle from the belly of the beast. Satan is laughing at my painful madness and aching, heart-wrenching pain, always laughing at my silence.

The chill of the morning dawn awoke me to the sharp pain of being busted over the head so many times that my eyes were filled with blood, my head meaning to be bludgeoned and bashed in my living breathing monsters of the night, sending splitting pain shooting through my skull. A deep rage and anger filled my spine and fists with this urge to get up and fight, and if necessary, to get up and kill. There was the moist smell of earth's soil and the damp cold morning dew in my clothes. The pounding in the back of my head had obliterated my senses of life and love. I felt as cold-blooded as the cotton-mouthed water moccasins down there in those swirling muddy waters, beckoning and calling and pulling me to its center, but the center of what? Something else was the center of everything and everywhere, and she was lying beside me. Frustrating anger and obsessing desperation have taken its toll on my psyche and body power; the monsters of the night underestimated the tormented soul of someone who is already dead.

Oh, how I died and died, again and again. I don't even have to breathe like a snake, and my heart barely pumps the cold blood through in chills of the spirit world's gazes and whispering observations. I can hear them all whispering, calling me back out of my hibernating transformations. The eternal gaze of the endless ancient wanderer has taken me through my inner planetary eye and far into the sun's rays of another realm. The dead that stand all around me and circle me with protection are the same among those who drift further out in either fear or amazement. The sun rose on our lifeless bodies and the coolness started to evaporate with the rising sun, drying the coagulating blood into cracks and dust to dust we lay. The inner anger that stewed within me for her won't allow me to bless this earth with my organic matter, and so as the pain shoots down my back and the muscles scream and joints ache, I push myself up desperately looking for her. If I was to open my mouth and call her name out loud, my heart will spring to life listening for her response, but this is what I must do, not bearing the thought of seeing her lifeless body in a harmful way. The very torment of it all is the thought she will not answer back.

Everything comes to an end, a cold bitter end; any warm loving end is reserved strictly for a small fraction. This is life, cold, cruel, unforgiving, and relentless. Storms come as they always do to wash up the slugs on your back porch and all the dead wandering eyes in your direction, and when they do, I'll be out there in the shadows with them watching your face as it realizes that one sacred thing. The one sacred thing drags all the scars and bruises to a bloody end, and you're the center of it all, as I am in agony and torment for her, so you shall be when this big cold, cruel world comes crashing down and all around you like the cold large raindrops from the punishing doom from up above. I used to look down at my boots waiting to see the rotten hands of the undead pull me into the mud and claim me as one of theirs. Someday when the thunder roars for you as it has done for me, then perhaps you too will see the undead clammy claws stretching to get there and grasp on you and pull you far, far down into the laughing skull's face, grim reaper's sweet embrace. We all have the option to give death a sweet kiss or stab back at the fucker like a pissed scorpion in the hands of the enchanted medicine man. My inner anger and rage is festering out of me like a flock of crows trailed by millions of pissed-off psychotic rabid mad bats, ready to fill your head with their ravenous screams. My blood is turning cold as I taste my own blood in my mouth; I feel my cold beating heart drop, and cold chills run down my spine and arms, these bloody mitts of mine. Did I get them dirty? As I wonder the thought, I answer back to myself, for her, yes, yes I would. The angels pour wine, Valkyries in Valhalla fill the drinking horns with honey ale… Oh, yes, yes indeed, you better bet your life I will kill for her.

The primal wolves' vicious snarls are in my calculating eyes. The soaring falcon overhead soar proudly like a faithful scout under the dark rolling thunder clouds. I stand up, becoming a beast as I frantically and cautiously ignore my aching heart. Where is she? Under the long weeds in the ditch six feet to my right I feel and sense what I refuse to see, yet I know I must go there and be destroyed back into madness and torment once more. Eventually even the bravest of hawks and eagles must leave the dead for the dead, for it creeps and waits and creeps and waits. The earth's scavengers are all closing in on what we all are, just another bloody extension to Mother Earth, a dropped rotten apple in the moist orchard floor. I cannot bear to see the face of an angel tainted by the ants and bugs. As my heart sinks. I know that is what I must do to see her beautiful spirit if she dared so to linger, and so I linger and listen as I slowly walk in a dizzy daze closer to her bloody body discarded like the very empty beer cans and burned roaches and cigarette butts, down there in the cold muddy wet ditch with tangles of overgrown back-wood weeds. Old country in its old twisted country roads, where sloppy, slow, bumbling bumblebees barely stay afloat in the humid summer sun. Down below them where the centipedes crawl was a gentle sleeping angel never to awake on this earth again. I knew as I stood over her my tears would help the rain wash the blood off and away downstream.

Somewhere close along Devils Creek, the psychotic paranoid delusions were waiting to grab me from behind and pull me far, far away with her. I refuse to believe she was there at my feet, under the wet rain as my face and skull ached and pounded. My fingers reach down to her pale white neck to touch her cold skin, and as my heart sinks as I feel no pulse, the tears fill my eyes as I know I must turn her face over to satisfy those questions that would otherwise haunt my soul. If the angels would drop from the sky now to take me, I fear I would not allow them without her. So as the tears fall, so does the rain drenching us under the god's lightning as I turn her head to face mine. The weltering swollen heart has four chambers and wind in the sails of ancient wooden ships that blow us all far away to strange distant places filled with strange distant strangers, all wanting to ease the pain of eternal torment and confusion. Strange and weird, this cold cruel world. How heartless is the devil's laugh and the creeping pan's distant flute, the cruel and unusual unfairness of being in human form.

The ultimate teacher of the time spent here is pain, pain, pain. I beg for mercy and receive none like a starving stray dog forgotten and unforgiving, lost and unfound. Is there love? Is there sweet admiring fairies and dwarves peeking from Witchwood's haunted eerie echoing forest, with smiles of hope and mercy, and if so, are they crying right now too? I cannot bear to try to comprehend what she went through or felt, and so I cast my gaze to the wood line where the hounds of hell keep a safe distance. The crows and ravens start to gather as all eyes fall upon the angel heart's narcissistic reflection, the rare sight of divinity in pain, unanswered questions from cruel actions. Then I realize I'm drifting back to that night once more, and it has long since passed. The peaceful feeling of being alone out in the country I will never know contently for I am too in tune with all the fellow lost spirits in mutual misery and despair, their eyes and their whispering voices always drawn to me, with an occasional one calling out my name, a blessing in disguise. The constant static of white noise tuning into the surroundings like supersonic rabbit ears linked to the manmade satellites lost in space set adrift to the gravitational pull of this spinning cold cruel world of Satan's domain, the devil's den. The gates of hell, as the locals call it, is a mecca of paranormal and supernatural occurrences that the old witch ley lines attract numerous varieties of the things from beyond that come to the ley lines illuminating energy like moths to flames. How can anyone that does not know how to lay low in a discreet manner ever understand that there is so much more out here in the unknown dark than their cell phones and TV shows? Perhaps I am an outcast rightfully so after all, a product of being the scapegoat who lost my only true savior, the savior and angel in human form so dauntingly stolen away from sight, sound, smell, and touch, leaving me only with fading memories like that old musty drifting rotting ghost ship in the foggy sea, the very ship that I am committed into following all the way down into the depths of Davey Jones's locker when the old cork-like drift wood becomes saturated enough to let go of sky and air and give in to Mother Earth's tugging heart. All that is left of my savior is but an old weathering tombstone, already stained with the weeds' moisture and left to be lost and forgotten by the ravishes of the forever time.

"I'm here, honey," she whispers, as I hear her voice loud and clear among the ancient souls of the spirit world. Thankfully being alone in haunting seclusion has spared me the embarrassment and refrained me of being able to answer back out loud, leaving only the unseen waiting spirits of the beyond to fill their longing of an old familiar tongue spoken out loud as a memory stimulant of what once was and will never be again. "Where are you?" I say calmly as the woods around spring to life, the rustling autumn leaves responding in anticipation in the cool dusks breeze. "Here," she responds in a teasing tone, "right here," and I turn to face what my body senses, the ice-cold anomaly of manifestation. I stare into her direction as the foggy cold ectoplasm mist starts to condense her in human form in front of my eyes, my exhaling breath almost matching her very apparition as the ice-cold void in her presence does the best it can with the energy of the witch lines. My heart is a tattered, discarded mess left behind a self-built wall to keep all the hateful vagabonds and riff-raff at bay. Hate and tough love has replaced the sweet mercy I've been robbed of, and my dull tired heart has accepted a world without love, a bitter resentment that longs for these silent times with just the two of us, briefly and temporarily separated by different realms of existence.

Spirit energy and everlasting and physical pain temporary clash and collide by only the truly enlightened who concern themselves not of the earthly material religion of wealth and objects. Surely there is nothing made of this earth, no mineral, metal, or cloth from earth or space that I can take with me; there is nothing anyone of us here can take with us but our everlasting souls of reanimated pain, refried horror echoing its cold grasp from beyond the grave. Knowing this I realize in a humbled, grateful way how lucky I am to still see that she is only here for a while, to leave a message, say a long goodbye, and be released into the warm sun that patiently waits with visions of a better life. Down here in the eerie silence of the haunted Witchwood Forest, she appears to me in a way that only spirits and ghosts can see, but to a normal content mortal soul, it would look like a crazy person talking to an imaginary foggy mist that is nothing and no one. I watch her face take shape in a blurry old memory that sorts out the still recognizable things of her personality as she whispers, "Don't you see? Do you see yet?" My tongue ties in knots as I swallow gulps of cold air. I know she is giving me closure, but I also remind myself that patience is virtue, and so I listen intently and motionlessly, hoping and praying my worst creeping nightmares of paranoid delusions do not come tapping me on the shoulder to confront my denial. The initial shell shock of traumatic events leave me paralyzed with fear and speechless with deep thought. All the what-ifs fly around my head like the last insects of fall to reawaken old suppressed and unwanted memories, the scars of the wounds that time could forget but never heal, the shocking realization of some sort of dreaded paranoid thought that could actually be true, the final moments of demise, and how to wrestle with it and accept it as it truly is. I look at her in intense silence, as I let her into my soul and troubled heart as I whisper back, "See what, my love? Who did this to you?" I feel the cold empty space in which she manifests touch my face, then pass through my body and fill my empty aching void within. There deep within the sorrow and despair of falling up and flying down, she fills my mind with the painful flashes of that night we were attacked by some unknown evil in human form—the things she remembered that I could not. It was more painful than what I so desperately tried to forget, the splitting aching pain in my skull as I feel the blood blind my eyes and trickle into my mouth, her screams and calls for help as the frantic panic takes hold. There was a helpless feeling of being trapped and unable to defend the very thing that is most important, the reflection of love lost in some sacred chapter to a musty moldy book in the dusty mildew corners of dirty spiderwebbed cellar floors.

The house will always eventually crumble on top, entombing the answers for all time, the old foundation still accompanied by the unnatural flower bed among the weeds on the forest floor. Why on earth does the closure have to hurt so much, and why does the world watch the lonely unknowing discarded soul suffer stranded, like some lunatic lost? The reasons are all before me in her searching eyes almost faded into a blurry fuzz of faded lost emotions, a poison digested like a holy hit of high-powered LSD. A deep mind-expanding knowing of senses and unspoken, untold, unsung feelings from the eyes of the amazed wanderer. She is the reason for this dark seclusion; she has always been the reason, and here she is before my blessed gifted eyes still soothing the eternal black hole of pain with her unearthly presence, the apparition of all my heart ache and gut-wrenching insanity slowly filling that empty void within with her unworldly gifts by the welcoming goddesses of the lost netherworld. I can smell the fresh newfound love within her cold ghostly all-seeing and all-knowing newfound wisdom. The tears that swell in my eyes are the aftermath of realizing how unworthy I am to have such a gift. If only I could hold her, hug her, embrace her, but she is still soothing the hole and empty space within by some cool misty fog of healing mercy. The images she pushes in my mind as I struggle with the realization that this too shall pass and end are both an overwhelming stir of distant refreshed memory and emotion that swells within my heart like ancient typhoons on native islands. The ecstasy of true love, the satisfying healing fulfillment of loves hearty potent power has finally came to offer mercy and warm kindness from under the weedy spiderwebbed graves of haunted energy and faded eerie silence. The window to the soul on a dark and dreary stormy morning drained and stained, yet the pain remains, and here she is once more within me as she always was, to give me the peaceful serenity I so long for. The flashes of that night come to me in torturous painful detail, and as the tears fall, I feel the remedy of love take hold. They say the truth shall set us free, even from the most fearsome realizations from the darkest scariest thoughts that we all shamefully push back into the corners of our minds. The truest, sincerest love from an ancient endless heart has the wisdom and forgiveness to find, see, and cure insecure thoughts and emotions. Fearful paranoid delusions of suppressed memory are revealed as the crippling parasites they are.

She flashes every memory and painful feelings of sorrow and confusion that I hid in the darkest corners of my insane mind and forces me to confront them in loving understanding, until she brings me to the one in denial, the most haunting memory that I brainwashed myself into dismissing as just random repeating nightmares. As all the shocking heartbreaking truth unfolds from my tangled mind, I feel her step backward out of my restored body and stare me into my eyes, a sweet soft smile of an angel and a gentle kiss on the lips. She steps back and smiles, as I realize I am seeing her just as she was, no longer as a misty foggy apparition and once more in true physical form. The dark thunder clouds overhead make way just big enough for a small ray of sunshine to part through the dark purple and blue psychedelic kaleidoscopes of the eternal echoing wall between her and my world. A sudden feeling of jolt shocks me into the ever so present realization of the same feared thoughts I so closely guarded in paranoid denial. The memories unravel and the painful bitter truth sets in as I watch her forgiving loving smile turn into tears, and I know the sobering reason as to why. It was I who was bludgeoned to death by the two monsters of the night alongside my lost angel, and from a bird's-eye view, I am thrown back into that cold, cold morning in the weeds on old Devils Creek's graffiti-covered bridge.

I am drifting slowly upward as I see both of our lifeless bodies lay below. I feel a familiar comforting hand grip tightly within mine and turn to see her smiling face. I was a lost wandering soul not truly aware that I departed this cold cruel earth, and she watched patiently above with painfully intent precision, ever so keeping a watching eye on a lost soul trapped in the beyond realm of the spirit world. With the sincerest granted permission of the weeping and concerned Valkyrie angels up high in Valhalla's great halls of heaven, she was allowed to watch over and retrieve me herself and carefully wrapped me in an alternate fantasy world to let me work out my pain and heartache. She walked patiently beside me in the graveyard to let me know and see easily in her gentle merciful way while I worked out my confusion, denial, and sorrow. When the moment of truth was upon me, the heaven's gates of Valhalla shined through the thunderclouds for sweet mercy and understanding, with her riding the powerful sun rays all the way down here in the haunted Witchwood Forest to scoop me up like a proud Viking left behind but never forgotten. What of old realms and dimensions never spoke of and hardly seen? Alternate universes and the astral projective spirit world? Merely cocoons of transformations into a higher state of being—down here we are brutal and primitive, but facing that primal existence, we become more evolved in a universal empathy of love and respect for those deserving. What is really love but a simple admiration in the eyes of another—ever so changing and the apple of the eye who appreciates the nourishing effects of what another soul can offer.

I was a lost wandering soul in the valley of the trapped souls, such is purgatory, a place as ancient and ageless as the secret supreme knowledge of forever time. There are so many questions that go unanswered, but none of that matters now, as long as I was with her again. The dark, dreary, foggy realm of Witchwood Forest is none other than Helheim, an ancient purgatory, sometimes even more gloomy, a last stop for lost wandering spirits. My sweet lost love who loved life so innocently and wholeheartedly, has become my Valkyrie, my angel, my savior, cleansing the pain with sweet, loving mercy. My lost love I longed for down here lost within Witchwood for many mad seasons of dismaying sorrow and desperate despair, left alone and far behind with a bitter antisocial loner. I am dressed in the old goth and stoner wear of tradition; the uniform of angry rebellions were usually the good old long black trench coats, black leather coat, long chain wallets, spikes, piercing, tattoos, the old faded holey blue jeans, blue jean jacket and flannel shirts. A stoner or misfit can easily spot one from the other. I never knew why I've never seen my fellow freaks in the mortal flesh while I was wandering the twisted trees and sticky poison oak vines surrounded by sticker bushes and all the other weeds that like to cling, grab, scratch, and leave a piece of 'em behind tangled in your socks or jean bottoms.

I wonder in painful solitude; if she is indeed one's savior and merciful release of all this horrific heart-aching pain, then could she equally be a tormentor and trickster in a seducing, sly way. No way, not my baby. No way. My stained sorrow promises more cold lonely tomorrows, and no warmth of love can follow as I stumble on the cold damp ground feeling empty and hollow. Laughter echoes and haunts old Witchwood's treetops as they twist and turn upward into the full-moon night of suspicious shooting stars and strange UFOs that sprinkle the starlit night sky like snowflakes floating through the cemetery courtyard. I used to see the character that was myself as I imagined how I once looked like, and that astral projection of my doppelgänger would suddenly manifest and appear in broad daylight around other souls without even being seen or detected. I would wonder if anyone could see this figure in black as I did, long trench coat and dark hood, or was I the only one who could see this younger former version of myself in some cold lost realm of depression and silent solitude. And as always, just as I wondered these questions along with the main question of where did this manifesting apparition come from, I always forget to not look away for too long, for as soon as I did, the figure in black would no longer be of avail, nor any rhyme or reason for the purpose of his presence be explained in logic as it would once again disappear as quickly as it appeared. Apparitions of unexplained nature always seem to manifest in the same place, and so did my own doppelgänger of a younger former self, just up on the high ridge of Witchwood cemetery near her resting place, rested upon her headstone cold to the touch, with the same year of her death.

My heart always sinks low, as I bring you to the end of this short haunting tale of dreadful doom as I realized now as you will with me that I have been haunting my own self out here in search of her distant spirit drifted in and out of thin walls of the spirit world. I know the answers of this lonely haunting down below the hill into Witchwood's Devils Creek, and *them* and *they* have gathered among the pagans and occultists calling on the very father of darkness lingering about in sunless lightless, heartless dreary days, where the forest floor sees no sun rays and the eerie silence holds no laughter or sounds of animals plays, just the cold sinister sorrow of depression's dismal daze of a sight of night that sees the inside fright and reveals it beyond that gaze. A twisted trail weaves through the thorns and vines like nature's creepy maze. Oh how mundane and repetitious tears can drown years and fears to change its ways. I see her walking into the distant setting sun as springtime's floating flower pollen gently dance around her shrinking departing image with the softly spoken words whispering into the sweet-smelling breeze among the headstones that still carries a faint hint of her unique scent, reminding me of mixture of her perfume and laundry detergent with the words "Don't leave" as she shrinks into the springtime horizon.

"Don't go," I hear myself whisper under my breath as my heart seems to be pulled in her departing direction. People were not meant to be alone; we were meant to connect, to comfort, and to love with the healing power of listening and understanding instead of speaking and demanding. If you are running or just standing, look at what life is handing and follow what your heart may be planning. Down there somewhere, anywhere but here, beneath my feet, beneath yours, beneath all of our feet is an ancient world stained with the blood of our forgotten ancestors that cry up from the sweet smell of dirt. In summertime, nighttime summer scent of rich soil and the wild weeds that grow from the fertilized dirt of all dead organic matter, I wander lost in what the natives called the spirit world. I remember seeing a younger version of myself that no one else could see, appearing randomly at certain places and certain times but in no particular order, the long black trench coat with the old holey worn-out hoodie underneath, with the hood drawn over his head, or was it my head as this apparition of my former self was only seen in the thin air by my haunted eyes only. I remember telling my dear love to not go and to not leave me, but seeing my former younger doppelgänger in some spiritual apparition was just a simple clue by a higher almighty, all-knowing, mercifully loving creator, a god among gods and goddesses, an all-seeing all father who held compassion for the wounded, for the broken hearted, and for the scarred and torn within.

Tattered and battered battle flags blow in the rain, waving in the cold gray lost days that we all pretend do not exist as we all pretend there is nothing to complain about along with all these lonely, depressing heartaches that long to be released, tugging at our heartstrings like a ghost of our former selves. I'd tell my sweet love of my life to stay with me. I'd whisper out loud to her ghost, "Don't leave me, please stay," but she would come and go in the same manner as my residual doppelgänger of a former younger self in my prime of physical and emotional strength. Vanished, disappeared in thin air, and not a single fellow living soul around me ever took notice, not even in the slightest attention of curious disbelief and confused bewilderment of the supernatural and paranormal spirit world that I thought was just merely all around me in some thin air that was thicker and more humid in some ulterior motive, in some multiverse, inner dimensions of monolithic magical marveling amazement that enchanted the gifted who could see and hear what was not only beyond the graves of our loved ones and even the graves of our own selves but even beyond the realms of this earth and this world as we know it, as we perceive it, or even more accurately put, as we all *think* we know and perceive it, in which we all perceive things differently in our own unique, weird, strange ways as we are the animated bodies of our own universes. We recognize ourselves as unique stars, as different as each single star in an endless ocean of astral stars shimmering out there beyond the summer night skies.

With a crushed beer can and a loud belch, my wandering eyes scan the universe over head up there in the deep dark night sky as I toss the empty can in the ditch with all the other cans and bottles of all those before me. Maybe down there among all the crushed cans filled with ants and centipedes was an empty can that my sweet soul mate held in her soft, delicate tiny hands as she laughed and giggled in oblivious wonder at those same stars, those same stars that we must realize we are before we can understand the concept that we are walking, talking universes mingling with thousands of other universes. When her universe looked through her beautiful round eyes and stared into my universe, somehow the very space in between pulled us closer like the heavy zero mass of black holes pulling us closer together to gaze into each other's dancing, smiling eyes, a place where neither one of us could run or hide. With that kind of magical spark that ignites the beating heart, it's easy to confess an age-old inner question we all ask ourselves and rarely ask another, and that is, How are we supposed to contain such ancient powerful emotions? How are we supposed to keep it all inside? Those imploding stars and expanding universe swell our hearts with the trade winds that fill our sails to explore and go further than just what we see and feel, but what exactly is past that horizon in the nighttime skies? Where does that old country road under the full moon and shimmering stars go? Up over those dark treetops just behind the treetops' skyline is the soft glow of my little hometown, and with her hand in mine, we go further past that old familiar glow. We explore like two lost satellites that escaped orbit and drifted with the rogue shooting stars in burning iron meteors of spells that can't be broken by the powerful magical worlds of destiny and realms of fate.

All good things must come to an end, all good songs must come to an end, all good journeys must come to an end, all good loves must come to an end, all good stories must come to an end. It's not easy to face the end, but with every end comes a new beginning. The beginning of this story is a purgatory type of realm, a waiting room of spirit worlds, somewhere down beside that old creek in Witchwood. Devils Creek is the cocoon where the painful life lessons of love and loss, joy and sorrow and wise understanding are only learned too late in a body more weaker and fragile than our former strong and beautiful younger selves. The youth we burn away for knowledge come creeping along in the dark hours of lonely aging solitude, and these lessons learned in this life are just the caterpillars crawling into their cocoons to sleep a restful easy slumber among the stars in some waiting room of realms beyond our understanding.

Purgatory-type spirit worlds are described in different religions but all hold the same description. The foggy lost cold damp swamps of Hela's Helheim or a place between heaven and hell as described in the church where what we perceive or think we know of the living have a free-will duty to remember us and say a prayer to help us break out of the cocoon and watch the budding rose on the rose vine open up and bloom with the scent of a brand-new fresh flower for those good old sloppy clumsy bumblebees to collect pollen under that perfect blue sky and golden sunrays that give warmth and sunlight to the towering looming bright yellow sunflowers in the backyard of hers and my nest house with a perfect backyard for a picture perfect home in a perfect love. The slow-creeping gray thunderclouds in the distance striking lightning come slowly rolling in with heavy cool winds to wash away the sunshine, and with its fury of thunderstorms and tornadoes, perfect homes and perfect lives are ripped apart. Alone I walk out the back door after she was taken from me that horrible night, I walk under the cold gray skies and see all the nests the storm blew out of the trees along with the dead fragile baby birds already crawling with scavenging insects, dreams to fly from the nests of proud parents coming to an end.

I look back over my shoulder from the end of my property line from my backyard and see an empty lonely house, and as I stare into the dark windows under dark skies, I see her ghostly silhouette of her outline staring out the window at me. She comes and goes at certain windows, at certain times in no particular order. I can only hear her voice out there in Witchwood Forest, where the tragedy of the storm's violence within the troubled hearts of lost mislead souls who contain within dark turbulent universes still in the Big Bang stage, not yet matured enough to have stars or planets, just the dark empty eyes of the great white sharks who stole my baby out there in Witchwood, only to be buried in the same old unkempt cemetery just a mere heavy stone toss from the bloodstained country road that touches some of the borders of the graveyard.

My cocoon is that of a suppressed memory, of a suppressed nightmare, so horrid and brutal for me to face or recall that my mind forces a different personality of what may be a few to shut down the scared, confused, lonely, distraught me and take over with a different personality that locks away those memories from my own self and guards them with distracting cryptic words of deep thought to force even those who dare to be inquisitive of me to have their curiosities altered to new subject matter, of zero matter, or does it matter? Which proves my point, the sleeping caterpillar is me, and Witchwood Forest was a realm left behind in some kind of dream state. Astral projections sleep well in an altered state of being, as the Devils Creek is the cocoon. This life I had to live is the life we all were forced to live. We are not perfect, no one is, yet we long for perfect lives, and when we are cut, bruised, broken, and beat down, the scars still remain, and they tug on old dull achy heartstrings and echo mournful tears of sobbing sorrow within old tired souls. You see, this is where I leave Witchwood Forest behind in your arms and in your heart, because these where just the last thoughts fading away in a dying man's brain on last breaths. My sight has become a weird tunnel vision as I watched helplessly as my love lay dying next to me on that old hard blacktop alongside the gravel and overgrown weeds in the ditch. I remembered the happy times we shared, and I held on to them.

I could not let go as my personality split into multiple personalities to fit the multiverse of many different realms, dimensions, monoliths, ley lines, and spirit worlds. She never died; she lived on and came out of her cocoon a beautiful new living radiant, shimmering love that shined life on everything she saw and touched. She changed so many lives. Every person she met she touched in a spiritual way. It was I who exhaled my last breaths out there on that dark old country road. My eyes wandered at the growing puddle of blood that slowly seeped out of me and drizzled in slow growing pools that stained the weeds as it drained in the ditch behind my head. Her apparitions, her occasional voice, these glimpses of her that I caught once in a while was not me seeing her as she appeared to me in some ghost form. But rather, it was her seeing me in my ghost form, the very ghost form that could not let her or our life together go. Oh, how it slowly slips through my cold fingers too frozen to clench a tight grip, my grasp slowly letting go. Everything and anything, familiar songs she sings, certain memories she brings, all are slowly slipping out of my reach as my thoughts and memories come to close an end, and my mind goes back even further before we ever met, before I ever fell in love with her, before her universe looked into mine. There was another space and time swimming through an old ancient oxygen, calling me to collect the memories I wasn't supposed to forget, gather, rather than scatter, calling me to come in some numb sum, calling me to recount and recollect memories that refuse to be forgotten. As the fallen apple on the forest floor becomes rotten, as so do our bodies when we leave them behind like a discarded cicada skin mold, a snakes skin on an old tree branch, a dusty cobwebbed whispering relic of what was once a strong web with the once living spider existing as a spider.

We exist as human beings, and like a discarded used cocoon still stuck on the branches of the still growing tree, we must leave our organic bodies behind, our organic bodies that we spent most of our lives misusing and abusing in some form or another, leaving behind what at one point in time many centuries ago a purer clean version of potential fertilizer than our now toxic poisonous forms of being matter that we are now made of. Living, eating, drinking processed toxic poisons our whole lives as the mere trials and hardships of life in general break us down, spiritually, mentally, and emotionally that we no longer care if we are poisoning ourselves. No one wants to die, yet we all subconsciously speed up the process with drugs, alcohol, and unhealthy toxic impurities we carelessly put into our own private personal universes that has been referred to as our temples. Everyone wants to go to what they perceive as heaven, but no one to die to get there. When I died, I learned all these strange facts, and we all die. When you die, your body, whether fit, young, strong or fat, unhealthy, old, and weak, must be given naked to a stranger to detoxify the poisons you put in it your whole life. Cremation kills all diseases and toxins, unless you get bled out and embalmed and dolled up to chase away the blue skin and purple lips pack to a reg-ular more familiar complexion to be put on display in a box. Unless you are unclaimed, unloved, or there is simply just not a funeral in your budget, then it's just stick a bone in your ass and let the fucking dogs drag you off. We are all born into the grave. You come out of the cocoon helpless and crying, and we all shed that aged version of that tiny former selves we all were and leave it behind in the care and possession of strangers, undertakers, morticians. The last thoughts in our unique individual brains slowly fade away as the magnetic electric spark of magical enchanting animating wonder leaves our lifeless, motionless bodies behind. Death is just a caterpillar entering into a cocoon; we are just transitioning into something new, strange, different, yet so strangely familiar—déjà vu. Just like it's all been said and done before; we have all been here and there before.

The End

DEVIL'S CREEK

Thank you for letting me go crazy.
But it's all water under the bridge now.

I STOOD OVER the bridge staring down over the edge into the dark murky undertow of Devils Creek and then eyed the trail leading down into Witchwood Forest and knew it would take me deeper into their haunted woods alongside the muddy banks. I can still hear the local town folks' persistent same old questions, over and over, "Where do you fish?" And of course, the same old questions about just exactly where *was* Devils Creek? How do you get there? The last I checked, I am not the keeper of Devils Creek, nor am I in a cult. So why was I always given the third degree on that fucking bridge and that old twisted haunted creek? The answers would eventually come, but they were equally if not more disturbing than the locals' infatuations with it. There is an age-old question that seemed kind of stupid to me: if a tree falls out here in this eerie heartbreaking silence, would anybody hear it? Let me improve that question with a more deeper insight—what if it was I *or* you were dead? *Or* better yet, if *I* was dead and this was all some limbo matrix purgatory, and then during a slow awakening awareness, I was indeed dead, and none of this was the real world I was born into. And then in the middle of this awakening, I wrote a book about Devils Creek while I was occasionally seen at Devils Creek (occasionally spotted by fellow deceased dead people here and there, asking me questions only a dead person would know to test and see if I, too, myself was also aware I was also dead). Then, would it matter if I wrote a book about Devils Creek? *And* even more questioning…would it ever get read? I think one day when I wade out until my nose and eyes become even with the part of the surface that meets some of the rays of sun that hits it between swaying summer breezes that blow lazy moths, dragonflies, and sloppy June bugs across its murky, muddy surface, below where the water gets a little bit cooler because it's too early in the spring for the sun to warm those depths, catfish swirling between my legs, I will let this book go to float up to the surface and let the water fade the ink until it runs and washes out of the paper and float downstream with whatever else was thrown in that sinister old creek, aside from empty beer and whiskey bottles.

Somewhere out there, someone knows something that is kept secret out of dreadful fear of angry spirits. I have always been intensely disliked as a person, so much in fact that most of the local churchgoing town folk wish to avoid me. I've stared into the deep abyss of darkness for so long that I have become stained with it, and the dark aura that follows me like a malevolent shadow person from the depths of hell would make most people follow that instinctual directive. I was once told that it is better to be feared than scared, and so I learned to accept the benefits of being a creepy misfit. But what does being creepy have anything to do with Devils Creek? Guilty by association? Just being the creepy guy that most of the hypocritical churchgoing folks gossip about is enough to be the prime suspect to any mishap. It may surprise you to learn that people would rather judge what they don't understand than take the time out to understand what they are unaware of and their own selves. While this may sound like something from the Salem witch trials, believe it or not, it is completely still present to this point in time. I died very young, but my body kept growing and aging. No one saw this but me, for it was my way of perceiving time as a lost soul, but what was completely unaware to me was everyone else saw me as that very child, the things people would say that would confuse me. Standing in the checkout aisle at the grocery store, the clerks would ask me, "Why aren't you outside playing?"

The most bewildering yet common memories of past lives are those that are unconsciously stored in the darkest corners of the mind because those memories are revealed in very subtle ways, like a familiar smile on a familiar face on someone you don't know or can't remember. People would ask me all the time, when was I going to leave my hometown? I used to take offense to this thinking, that they didn't want me until it occurred to me that there was no hometown in the first place. It wasn't that I couldn't leave, it was that I was scared to leave because it was a safe comfort zone in a happy memory, and so I was sent my family tree to be observed by a messenger from the other side. That very family tree vanished and was gone without a trace, because it was simply a clue from a family member that was not on the same plane as I was, and that clue was the people I thought were on this plane with me were really not here, and those whom I thought were not here are actually close by watching over me. And as I sit on the old aging log rotting away on the muddy banks of Devils Creek, in my lonely silence, I recall those memories of being down here with my loved ones still alive and full of life and wonder, and now, I must confess that those different planes of existence that I either cannot cross over because I have to earn my way across or because my own fear holds me here. These are not just mere planes, but the different worlds of the living and…the dead.

I stare into the shimmering, waving surface of Devils Creek's waters, knowing what lies beneath those murky undertows of nothing specific or anything other than people's guilt and shame. The old creek takes those guilty shameful things into her belly like a hungry snake and sheds them downstream like unwanted skin, and I, the lost poet, will never write a poem sweet enough to send me an angel. Those dark woods of Witchwood Forest are only filled with one thing to keep my lonely solitude comfortable, and that is the empty forgotten echoes of laughter and amazement running through the weeds and playing in the mud puddles as the adults stood on its muddy banks and fished. I could never bring back those smiling faces no matter how long I sat here and waited on this cold moldy log. Soon the night would fall, and the surface of the water would light up with fireflies and the stinging bites of mosquitoes as I wait alone for them to never return. I dream of them, and I dream what I would say to them, how I caught the most fish and drank the most beer and smoked the most pot under these huge shady oak trees covered in poison oak vines. I can't wait to go home and sit underneath the fan as Mom cooks and cleans to KSHE 95 on her crystal meth, and Dad is out in the shed toking on his weed, but I am content sitting here with my siblings watching cartoons.

A long journey has happened as the world around us dies, and those things of memory are all that is left in an aging body. I sit here under this bridge waiting for the familiar roar of car tires riding over the bridge, off to some wild and free road party to kiss and hold that girl who was so excited to wait for me. Those smiles are like angels' tears in the moonlight, as the earth takes back our bodies and our souls fly free like clumsy bumblebees in empty fields, no one knowing what happened. I wonder now as I sit out here in this dark forest if not knowing is easier than knowing, the dull aching pain within, of wanting and longing to see that smile of excitement on her face again but never will again. What did you do with your time on this earth? I stumble upon the overgrown weeds that covered the steep hill up out of the woods away from the lonely silent bank and onto the still warm country road with my ears filled with crickets and frogs chirping to each other in the night. I look to my left and then to my right and see not one headlight, but I do see something laying under the moonlight in the middle of the road, something discarded by that passing doppelgänger of my younger former self, tail lights disappeared into the distant darkness long ago to meet her as she waits with that anxious smile. I step closer until I am standing above it, looking down at it, and I reach down to pick it up. It is dirty, torn, and ragged and run over by long-gone passing cars. It's a tattered, battered rag doll, bound and used, a broken tool unloved and forgotten. It looked like it went through the ringer not only a few times, but it looked like it had been to hell and back and discarded like trash. A stepping-stone to reach a broken ring in the ladder and left there in the littered ditch with empty beer cans and other various trash.

Madness eventually turns into laughter because in this world there are no regrets, only time, ongoing moving time that never stops, and just a second can change everything. It can kill someone from the inside out, and all the tears and stories won't reverse it, fix it, or change it. "The angels are disappointed with you, Danny," a stern, cautious voice warns from over my shoulder. I turn to look, but no one or nothing is there; however the creeping realization slowly makes itself aware in my thoughts as my mind wrestles with the words and makes sense out of them. Yes, the angels are let down in a slightly annoyed manner, but nothing so serious I should be afraid, but the fact of the matter remains is I am stalling time by running from the bread crumbs of clues laid down to guide me to the real simple truth—painful truth and agonizing. Hardly seems simple at all when it is frightening and scary. I stall this precious time that could be spent with the ones I love because the strong physical reaction and self-awareness of the beauty and magical enchantment of life's equal awareness is gone.

I remember when everything in motion living and breathing and all around surrounding me from the gravitational pull of the spinning earth and the distance of the stars was all just as equally aware of me as I was of it—an energy that gave energy. Now it is all dormant, and the angels are slightly irritated. The one thing I must discover for myself, the one thing I must see with my own eyes and realize with my own mind might very well be the one thing that frightens me the most. The things that do not have basis in this current life yet echo from a far long lost forgotten life. Responses are put on pause by silent reasoning. Reactions of faded memories are still distantly calling for my dazed gaze to pay them attention one more time, even if it is one last time—the unmatched, unbalanced, emotional memory. Few people spontaneously recall any of their past lives. In fact, complete memory loss is typical for most people between lifetimes; however, I have died midlife many times. As I recall as a kid, the broken lines were read on my palm, broken lines in my lifeline. Memory loss plagues my confused mind and troubled heart because all the emotions surprisingly remain intact. Emotions seem to be a barometer for my sad trapped soul. It serves a bittersweet significant purpose in reincarnation. This may be my soul's way of preventing me from making the same mistake in some other distant lifetime. Avoidance can be one way to face a karma debt from a past life. Avoiding many times, souls become intertwined with each other for many lifetimes.

A destructive pattern in me that has developed over ageless ancient sorrow and traps the soul in this repetitive cycle. Souls in karmic relationships can also become addicted to certain patterns like vengeance and anger. I know my only solution and cure to this deep ancient despair is breaking the chain of repetition with forgiveness. Avoidance is just one way in which the correct reaction can be established. In the next lifetime, you may find yourself befriending this former enemy as you purposefully move the relationship into one of healing and facing the karmic issues between the two of you through a loving relationship. Past-life memories often are revealed to you through dreams. Haunting, taunting dreams of madness and sadness and horrific disturbing painful nightmares always bring me back through the old twisted woods of Witchwood Forest and Devils Creek. Winding, twisting knowledge is hidden deep into the sticks of the back-wood lowland flatland prairie, these old flat cornfields and wooded wild forests of southern Illinois.

This kind of dream is different from a typical dream, because there is a beginning, middle, and end. I commonly believed that somewhere on them old lost blacktop country roads with all their infamous painted bridges marked all the years you might've seen if there was just more time to do it all again, lost forgotten good times. The sacred celebration of everyone all numbing each other's pain, leaving all the shed tears behind and a shared happiness. Hugs and kisses all around, drinks are on me! Sweet thought alone down here under this dark cobwebbed bridge littered with shed snakeskin and decayed bones of the poor misfortunate critters who gave up down here in the muddy banks of the dark rolling undertow of Devils Creek.

Past-life dreams begin in the middle. They say you never know, and I strongly disagree. That is just the mimes and puppets mimicking my own body gestures and movements. I will always extend my hand in loving, kind gestures of friendship and common ground, but if you mimic me like a reflection in the moon in the surface of Devils Creek, then I will softly ask the demonic bitches below to pull you into the undertow with a sweet, soft kiss of deceiving passion. Into the arms of death, they will drag you into those rolling muddy currents of the fat lingering catfish. I will watch them pull you under as they did to me and maybe shed another tear. Each scale in the shed snakeskin draped under this old bridge cannot match all the tears I cried down here alone, far from any loving company. I will always miss you all, but what could any of you do for a lost, scared, and frightened kid trapped in a soulless, ageless ancient curse. I will weep for every last one of your smiles and sweet softly spoken humor that dried my tears to smiles. They say tears clean the troubled soul and quench the thirsty loneliness within. In a past-life dream, we can all suddenly find ourselves in the middle of a scene as though we all have stepped into a movie after it had been playing for hours in the dark. The tears fall again as I think of all the lovers and loved ones who sat next to me in that big dark theater ready to leave all their pain and sorrows behind for an hour or two to travel in the lost happy moments in our brains and be entertained by my fellow entertainers. We are all troubled souls, so my debt is this. I give you this story to help you find that lost pain within and that trapped soul we all had to leave behind when the big cold, cruel world came calling and demanding the best out of all of us. And so I rolled around all the roads all over the country and ended up in a lot of some of the weirdest little towns meant just for me. I always touched so many lives that truly needed my presence, which I always generously provide in the most sincere contentment and intention, but it only numbed my inner pain for just a small angel's tear or a god's wink. Events have already occurred, but you're confused and unsure what is going on. These dreams have no beginning or ending. They feel very real, and you can't believe it was just a dream when you wake up.

Probably one of the most profound ways to recall a past life is through lucid dreams. Have you ever had a dream where you were aware that you were dreaming? That's a lucid dream. For example, you may suddenly dream you're in the middle of a natural disaster in a place unfamiliar to you, yet in the dream you know where you are, you know where to go, and the people in the dream are also familiar. You view your dream as though you're watching a movie unfold, but you're an active participant, and in the spirit of morbid curiosity you can watch yourself play your role without hesitation. Another form of this memory is spontaneous recollection. The moment it occurs, you feel as though you've been thrown back into that lifetime and are reliving the events as they unravel as they once so strangely occurred. As one can only bravely fathom, there are many ways one can gain information about past lives and tap into those memories like a delusional matrix trip with all of its super weird glitches and giveaways, all telling you in silent hushes and quiet whispers to shut the fuck up and don't tell another living soul or suffer the stalking followers who sniffed you out and got hot on your trail. Past lives don't always flash in front of you like a TV screen. Sometimes those memories are held deep within your emotional well or in a cobwebbed wine cellar, waiting for you to duck your head down those old musty steps and pick out a favorite spirit from a favorite year and run with it.

Evil is what is morally wrong, sinful, or wicked. Evil is the result of bad actions stemming from a bad character, and all the rest is psychobabble from cleverly strewn words in the literal sense of any enlightened soul. Yet clever words do not make it true; clever words only help certain people see and set certain others free or in line to the right path of acknowledgment. Yet here we are together in some old wise tale of two vicious fighting wolves at each other's throat, a deeper look at the conflicts of the human heart, and the morbid delusions of tortured souls, intertwined in ancient and ageless sorrow. Sleeping always and forever is the space time that we all sleep within and have to face in our deepest dreams, ready to face the unknown and unexplainable with true vigil courage. Around me are my loved ones all laughing and giggling and taking those pictures, waiting for me to wake up from that deep sleep under the currents of life. Do not pull the plug. Wait for me as I sleep. Please do not give up on me until we are all gathered as one like some ancient tribe in the American West. When you know we all hear the same thunder roar and beating drum, then we have all gathered here in the same place, only then you can wake me up.

Dream big, old wandering one who feels no pain, because earth does not need you anymore. You have transgressed and transformed out of your cocoon and turned into the black hummingbird moth under the pale moon. Fly high, fly free, and never look back, just exist in your own weird unique way. If you land down here in the muddy banks of the Devils Creek, then I promise I will pour you your own little beer puddle from my bottle for you to land and take a sip and fly over that rippling scrying surface of calling spirits. Fly close enough to feel it, then fly far away to take it with you. The wonder of all creation in the splendid eyes of the beholder. I waited patiently as all them witches gathered around me, and I picked wisely whom I give my black mirrors to. Always give the kind, wise old witches a token of you to keep in good holdings, blessings, and tidings. If you don't understand why, then I must leave you to wonder, for some explanations are only self-known. The loving, adoring watching eyes of those who take pity on a soul are given a second chance, and the bewildered confusion of silence and deep thought do not match up with the regular outgoing social behavior of the normal bunch. The tough lessons for a soul are cast on this earth to learn the painful lessons of mortal compassion, the very compassion for those who will never let you fit in their cliques and circles.

You have to fight and fend on your own, receive no pity parties or sympathy fucks, and have to aggressively lock horns with every cocksucker asshole just to get a piece of ass from the blind does who really don't give a shit. Survival of the fittest—there is no room for weakness and consideration in a show-me and prove-it world. The actions speak louder than words to the lost soul who had to fight way too soon and grew tired way too soon because of it. The crippling, hobbled handicap realized the definition of insanity is attempting the same thing over and over expecting different results. There is final admitted acceptance of defeat and the pride of the lone wolf who has ran out of steam. Some things even Mother Earth respects enough to leave untouched and well enough alone are the bleached bones of our ancestors that pose as a cautionary territorial warning of trespass from beyond the grave. There is no sympathy for the shunned and blamed, no compassion from the selfish, envious gossiping masses; the packed vermin in their old haunted churches, their hypocritical whispers of ill intent and harmful wishes.

The painful lessons of humanity, some cleansing of the old ancient spirit in future lifetimes of false harmony, are all constructed by certain ways of prideful thinking and arrogant blind egos to escape the pain of the hectic chaos that patiently waits for you to forget it's there. Life does not want to knock you on your ass at your lowest and most humble state; it waits for you to get high and mighty first before it tears down the walls and exposes you for exactly what you are, not what you think you are. The hypocrite's failure to practice what they preach, the arrogant delusional who receive no mercy or kindness from the cold cruel world that left them so far behind—they all have a painful, hateful excuse for everything, and it has always been all my fault, nailed to the cross, the experimental lab rat and guinea pig who everyone watches suffer for amusement.

How can I walk through the gauntlet of cold shoulders and turned heads without getting tainted and stained with their germs and diseases? Not now or never will any mortal ever unlock my heart and release it from the chambers of my own rib cage; it is reserved strictly for the gods and Valkyries who always watched with gifts and clues to guide my steps down here in the valley of the dead. They are gathered like shadows in the twisted thorns and tangled brush of the lonely paths forgotten by the very ghosts who made them. Watching, whispering shadows on the air we breathe, the lone wolves test the winds scent for the direction of the hunt and the location of any threat. The hungry scavengers follow and lurk behind as madness comes to wash away the blood. My parasitic madness has washed away a lot more than blood; the painful affliction stains me, forcing me to walk around with it all over me like a dark dome filled with a cloudy menacing aura of gloomy doom for all the world to see, an unfinished spell that cannot be washed off or scrubbed clean by sacred spells or compassionate, merciful, unconditional love.

I walk into public places to confront the source of my deep-rooted agoraphobia, extreme anxiety, and hopeless lifelong addiction to Xanax, subtly scaring off all the scared, timid, and shy just enough to put an extra spring in the knees and pep in the step and scatter away in every direction. This was a lonely mundane repetitious existence of my little one-horse town and the frightened and disturbed state of mind of those who dared not confront me and avoided getting caught or tangled up in the web of any type of casual pleasantries or painfully hard-to-bear small talk that would drain my still young heart of self-coping hope and steal away my reassuring comfort and turn it into paranoid fears of conspiracy to fill the cold empty spaces in their zombie-like brains and cold, selfish hearts. This was the type of weird chain of reaction stimulant of weary preconceived notions of action that kept the strange town folk practically running, but being the only living breathing hometown celebrity who still occasionally resided in the old two-hundred-year-old buildings was not something they could celebrate loudly and proudly in boasting conversation in their late-night cliques and bar fly circles at all the countless bars all across the little town's late-night weekend scenes, with one advantage of where every person either sees me but are too shy to approach me or those who had met me, talked to me, or even sat next to me at a bar giving them a good story, certain stories that they would lovingly tell with humor.

The bittersweet curse of being too infamous of an American iconic living legend always made people ask me, Why did you move back here? There was the same look of confusion in every eye who asked that very same question. Sooner or later, when my whole "big fish in a little pond" existence became a routine of madness, then living in this way slowly wore down on my own paranoid, psychotic confusion, and without the help of fellow sympathizing kindred souls, it eventually became apparent in my mannerism and speech that I was surpassing the typical occasional delusions of grandeur and toppling down into the bottomless white rabbit's hole of full-on constant delusions—delusions that acted like a calculating reasoning for things either unexplainable or of things too shocking or embarrassing to believe. Upon this distance of point, from birth to the current point of now, there was a lot of ups and downs, and it always is with most people, of course some peoples' downs. Some of us who really know the true hardships of life can probably chuckle to ourselves as we ask ourselves, "Oh, is that all?" The tough old life of heartbreak and hardships of barely just getting by and all the endless variety of drugs we took to cover up the pain and laugh at it all eventually runs out along with the money and leaves us alone with nothing and no one, with a dull, depressing loneliness within that leaves an unbearable ache in the center of the soul and heart. The solution, if not a caring angel to be the understanding friend and companion we all long for? Then drugs, alcohol, and more drugs. Either way you cut it, it is a vicious relentless circle, and so I dream of days of young before the drugs have taken their toll on my poor confused, lost, bewildered pain-riddled mind with all of its painful madness, days of young happiness filled with love, wonder, and endless joy so content with the simple small blessings and wonders of life. In my lonely times of depressing agony, I ask myself… Where is my loving woman? Where is my happiness? Why do I linger in the lost happiest times in my life like a ghost in the dark? Down here under the old bridge in the weeds, watching the dark surface of the old muddy water flow on down to Silver Lake, I recall some of the most happiest times. Of course, not all the happiest times were down here, but any places or places you cling on to in dying, denying desperation. The eyes in the darkness watch in unnatural, malicious patience the prize, the payoff that gives worth to the wait. There are cries in the darkness of screaming souls being torn from the arms of Mother Nature and into the demise and ending thereof. Earth so giveth and so taketh away, so the weary, always-aware mind of brutal primal instinct keeps me alive and well, even if I myself is sadly am sitting on borrowed time. The darkest spirits still waiting on all of us patiently awaited our arrival. Destination has become seen in a dismal, dreary demise. Welcome to the black hole Witch Lines of Devils Creek…

When it's time to fall in eternal judgment, it is the simple spats and bickering of demons and angels who want to secretly fuck each other for being the opposite that they are forbidden to be, and high up ahead in the loud clapping of the thunder, God chuckles his hearty, slightly sinister laugh. Souls roll around like two giant hands in a jumbo barrel of grapes. Oh, how we make the sweetest wine from the sweetest time as our flesh ripens with knowledge. Deep within the sounds of chirping crickets and croaking frogs and slithering snakes came the roaring rush of the deep murky water below, constantly tumbling and rolling as the biggest catfish hold their ground. Somewhere down here in the damp cool darkness, I found my blood-type behavioral trait, the resentful pagan outcast forced to turn into the dark arts instead, a bitter resentment of being surrounded by arrogant, egotistical greedy, money-grubbing parasites of society. My misfit, loner outcast attitude became a badge of honor to my dark soul as I embraced the labels and, gratefully, the life that came with it. Antisocial tendencies became more and more dominant until the hate for the greedy parasites grew into a frenzied desire of vengeful bloodlust. Merciless and unforgiving are the enlightened to the parasitic army looking to pick your bones clean like an unholy alliance of hyenas and vultures and all the other creepy crawling critters that come following after. The dried bleached bones, brittle, cracked and rotting, are left out in the elements of the dead dry sun. Some centipedes and ants come too late, only to crawl by looking for earth's other fallen gifts, the fallen rotten peach with its fuzzy purple and blue toxic penicillin and stomach-turning mold. Rotting into the ground, just like me down here under the dark silent bridge in the night, too afraid to go stand up there on the old blacktop country road waiting for a passing car of drunk stoners.

A flicked cherry to the roach too short to pass, discarded out the passing window exploding like cherry-red fireworks in the pitch darkness. How many times was that me. *Or* was that me? Can I see all the bits and pieces of my wasted youth drag out into "good ole boy" ripe old age? Was this bridge over Devils Creek nothing more than crossing over to another existence or plane to another dimension of being? Here we *all* must return, no matter how arrogant or how humble. The mirrors eventually must be turned to you in the reflection of Devils Creek's old muddy, murky waters. The roaring, rushing underbelly of the beast beat and pulverize lifeless bodies and limbs into nature's bone breaking and bruising grinder, filled with all them slimy hungry catfish. Down there in the murk is death, and death is not as elegant on the eyes as blooming black roses are on a midnight pagan altar; death is macabre and disturbing as it haunts you instead of pleases. The toils and spoils of meth-burned foils and everything else are meant to get you high and tell society and reality goodbye. Oh, how we try to stop and admire all the beautiful small things that delights the heart, but sooner or later with time and pain, the heart grows heavy and runs from the tiny beautiful things and into the numbing pain of the reality of having to hide the addictive drug-abusing dope fiend from hell.

Drugs or reality? It hurts to say hello and goodbye to them both. The guilty conscience ends up echoing into a distant maniacal laugh deep within my mind, like the devil just beat the shit out of my little angel person on the other shoulder with the unsaid message "One more for the dark side." Damn that little laughing fucker, and the painful, irritating madness is the sinister laugh is only an annoying sound, not something I could pull out of my head and strangle with my bare hands, giving back my own insane maniacal laugh in return, suffering a stranded solitude deep in Witchwood Forest along the muddy paths and trails along Devils Creek that come with an adoring beckoning call in a form of a whispering voice silently blown into your ear like a gentle wish of loving encouragement. "Explore me, come take a look, what is beyond the beyond?"—the obsessing desire of the calling of the goddesses' beckoning from behind and in-between the trees waiting to seduce you in the audio pleasure of nature's symphony and presence in a spell of lonely entertaining lust. All those ex-girlfriends who were fine with a spot in the cornfield or tree line was the early angry wasted youth of stoner's way of good fucking. The old trail of empty beer cans, wine bottles, and distorted attitude and perception were the early on stoned youth's anthem. The children of the real hippies were born on new levels of under-standing, the second generation enlightenment.

Somehow we all were eventually forced to look down, and it was that forever downward look within that did all of us in. All the lost souls follow behind like one-track-minded zombies, with Lucifer humming along in contentment. Slowly dragging themselves in a slow, steady pace you cannot out run, one by one the gnawing zombies fall on top of you, doing their best to get one savory bite. Bitten by death's dead black festering bacteria, slowly making you just another brainless zombie like the rest. Hell's winged spawns fly away in demonic laughter, the point of no return. Sacred old muddy ground holds your primitive brutality wide awake and completely aware of all your surroundings. The antennae of the moth bounce off the overhead bridge streetlights in a cluster moth mosh pit. Down here there was a darker mosh pit of pissed-off venomous water snakes. I often wonder as I wander down here…who is afraid of who? Me or the snake? Never been bitten or stung by anything venomous to venomous blood of a walking corpse, and one should ask them-selves…what nutrients come from the soil that sprouts mushrooms and spores? More than you think, oh so much more. Nature always heals. The old ghettos of them old Mississippi river's missing win-dows, graffiti-covered dilapidated buildings ready to crumble in on themselves, all the pain, the hardships, and the bloodshed brought the claiming back with the outreached hands of vines and weeds and small trees.

The soul we drained of Mother Earth will never be missed, just gratefully forgotten. I recall once a random pot smoking with a pissed-off mountain climbing hobo who ranted on and on how "mankind is unkind man," some typical modern hipneck rapping on about mankind's cruelty and merciless lack of compassion? What of innocent sweet and pure love from long ago—that beautiful spiritual magic we all have numbed and killed with bitterness and hatred? Now when I recall the hipnecks, hipsters, and true old school hippies from the sixties to seventies, I'm thinking, wow, what a hell of a welcome wagon, a misguided pirate ship full of wasted heathens and hooligans who only know how to brutally take what they want. Of course in distant star-filled skies full of hope, those thoughts also become conflicting. When does the line of limit come to tell my brain to "get a grip, chill out, calm down, take a deep breath, etc." The asshole is the dumb fuck who loses their temper first. Did I ever mention down here in the musty, humid mosquito-infested Devils Creek that I do not like assholes? But hey! Who does, right? Yet everywhere you go, there is always at least one close by, just waiting to give some snotty, sarcastic one liner out of the side of their neck, pushing and testing your temper and patience. Some universal test of personal evolution watches for your reaction to action. Do I slam someone's head up against a wall like some ignorant savage or calmly confront the person face-to-face under the beautiful sun. As they say, in the hours toward the bitter, dismal end, cool heads shall prevail; if not, then surely an attractive fantasy to foolishly romanticize. Or do I just hammer smash pile drive a hard jab into said asshole's snot locker or grill? Then comes the gentle, calm reassuring voices of limits and patience and conscience calling you back as you drift too far into the darkness with all the bats that collected in your bell tower.

Ta-ta now, bon voyage, beautiful one. Don't stop to think now, keep trucking in the solitude of the eternal void that gives us all the beautiful shadows of the night. Let me dance on the air you breathe and spin soft, gentle circles of the forest breeze through your hair and beautiful face. I am always free, proud and Free, alive and fully aware, scouting over the shoulders of my loved ones like a proud raptor, bird of prey. These are not the sign of the times no more, those delusional conspiracies got lost on the blowing wind of a forgotten sunset years ago when you were just a baby. Now look around at the new-age population control—man-made, tailor-made diseases to thin the blind masses of herding ignorance, slowly migrating together in a slow death march to make more room for the money-grubbing greedy, selfish arrogance that looks down on me. You like we are the very filth that they are made up of. They hate us for what they are, dull, numb, fake smiling predators with huge kitchen knives behind their backs, waiting to get the first stab at you. Kindness is stared down upon as weakness while the heartless corruption in the soulless masses help the death machine kill each other off like a blood sport version of the World Series or Super Bowl. Every night the news spews out the wicked world's black smog from its exhaust fumes, replacing our precious beloved oxygen with its poison gasses from the bulldozer's forest-demolishing action, reaction. No real solution is ever presented down here in purgatory, only the money-making death machines drenched in the blood of the innocent and pure at heart. If a wise voice of deep-thinking, free-spirited enlightened souls on the verge of divine intervention and compassionate solution will be torn off this earth by some devious intent by the fat rats who make the cash off the death marches. I have truly wept in the darkest hours of self-realization to not only my own imperfections but to this tough old cruel world. The very tears of heart-wrenching sorrow are turned into an amusing commercial for the monkeys to screech and clap at between the time-consuming mundane TV shows to help you zone into a zombie state as your own very precious life is being wasted second by second, minutes into hours, closer to your earthly demise. My pain, and the world's pain, is a joke and a good laugh for those who speed up the demise of Mother Earth and all her beautiful unique creations.

Your time spent here on this earth is truly a spiritual, mental, and emotional learning experience, a lesson-learning eye-opening wake-up call in the form of a cure to your zombie disease. The state of oblivion that we choose to not have to see or think about the truth has been tapping you on your shoulder and tugging you on your shirt sleeve. When you finally take notice of the kindred pure at heart who sees the good in you that you have lost sight of, be prepared to be human enough to weep the tears that have been drowning your heart and dragging your soul deep into the eternal void of the dark abyss. This old ancient creek has become my abyss, an escape from the hateful, prying eyes of the judging cold-hearted monsters who are salivating and drooling to put you in the meat grinder for every fucking thing you own, have, and think. Down here in the poison ivy and sumac-covered logs rotting slowly back into Devils Creek's cold, damp muddy banks is her. It always comes back to her, the one project of another human soul that you would never give up on, even if it took all eternity to figure her out. Did she find me up there in Witchwood forest at the foothold of hell's gates? The gates of hell are guarded by far more than just the dreaded three-headed ravenous, vicious hounds of hell, and all the stalking, waiting demonic entities in the shadows down here are too much for any blind, insincere lost soul. They only feel the cold chill and run from it like frightened children.

Run, run away from the monstrous, hideous, malicious, insidious moving creeping darkness that never slows down, its steady stalking pace just following behind in the dark shadows every time you dare stop to rest. It follows and never tires, the darkness in the shadows that *will* eventually smother you in a tidal wave of unworldly wickedness and evil. It all depends on where those dark bat-winged creatures from the blackness of the abyss decide to carry you and fly you away. How long and far are you willing to go for the hell ride, tagging along of Satan's booze cruising. Lucifer's sweet lies are whispered in the ears of those who never know the difference, to sink the hook of hell's bottomless eternal void, self-indulging selfish pain numbing slowly, clouding my eyes in a foggy haze, anything *they* can do to make me lose sight of her lost soul, *or* is that the very purpose? The hellish torment of heartache and loneliness of being misunderstood by everyone but the very person who did, gone. What is gone? Nonexisting? These are the tough age-old ancient questions of the natives who rightfully enjoyed this land, these dark woods, and menacing creek with spiritual respect. Those natives who called down the thunder in this dark place are still drumming their war dances in my heart and soul. These are the indigenous people who the true savages called the savages, the blessed people of the sun on this old American soil who traded with the old world Vikings in an old worldly way of respect, long before the vermin came creeping in with lies and tricks, all dolled up in a fancy deceitful language, the new tongue of the darkness that only the true kindred free spirits knew to command a sit-and-stay at a safe distance.

Sudden sounds grab my attention because that is the divinity in it all, those few of us who are truly aware of not just basic awareness. Long ago, I recalled a sad depressing act of cruelty from a fellow long-haired stoner pal out on some lonely back-wood country road from after closing some lonely road house tavern with a good old-fashioned barfight followed by the words "Don't come back" by the pissed off bar owners. Obliterated drunk to the point of barely being able to feel the cool summer night air on a numb face, I watched my crazy friend shoot signs and random critters, such as possums and coons with his illegal hand-me-down pistol he got from one of his "bath-tub crank" meth-making biker friends. Came the stain of the death dance that would creep up on me more and more over the years as depression of a tough old world tightened its hold on my heart. The moment of the heartbreaking lesson that stuck with me in a disturb-ing fashion pasted away in the cracks of a broken heart like plaster putty over a punched dry wall in some old abandoned trailer wall that once held a happy family before drugs, alcohol, and unfaithful sexual temptation tore the family to shreds, leaving empty echoes among the cobwebbed empty rooms filled with floating dust particles of residual negative energy of heartache. The old rusty pickup truck came to a slow, easing stop as the headlights spotted a lonely stray dog enjoying the wild freedom of the night. Like most animals, the dog was frozen in the headlights as the ancestral wolf inside sniffed and tested the summer night air to see if we were friend or foe. The orders to roll down my window a little lower came from my twisted friend in a low menacing undertone as he extended his long arm past my nose pointing the pistol outside the window in the dog's direc-tion. The animal's instinctual feeling of dreadful doom took over as my eyes was about to unknowingly witness a kind of painful cruelty that would be forever stuck in the darkest corners of my mind. Immediately the dog's senses brought its head down, tucking his tail in between its legs as it nervously started stepping strangely in place followed by my demented friend's description in the same menacing monotone, "Do you see how it does that weird little dance like that? That is because it knows it's coming." and then the crack of the pistol rang my ears as the dog dropped into the weedy ditch in the darkness as the old rusty pickup started back up down the old twisted roads.

The death dance has always haunted me ever since, the moment of the final end which the begs the question in all of us: Will you go proudly with no fear? Or beg for more borrowed time as the death dance inside rattles like the tail of a rattlesnake louder and louder like a dope sick junkie fiending for the next fix of antivenom to silence the snakes rattle and wash away the venomous poison flowing in the collapsing veins of aching joints and painful, disturbing memories. Down here in the dark in the eerie silence of the element of night itself, the haunting memory of the dog is with me as I feel the painful feeling of dread and doom creep up on me, forcing me to ask the question if I myself am on borrowed time. Or have I already stepped through the moments of the empty hourglass in the grim reaper's hand and carefully accompanied by death in a sympathetic mercy, gently letting me fade away into the gray fringe of dusk's greeting of sweet beautiful night while somewhere the truth can surface out of the muddy banks like a wildflower for a beautiful hummingbird moth? A place that once held love and compassion and a sense of safety in a soul-soothing haven is now silent and barren as the old trails are taken back by the forest by the weeds and brush that take advantage of its nourishing sunlight that gently and briefly shines through the forest treetops. The footsteps of all those I loved are grown over and forgotten, the pain there of self-medicated through years of drug abuse of all the most potent and dangerous available, anything to mask the pain. The unfortunate dilemma of numbing the pain is, it always returns in a slow, creeping squeeze, tightening its grip around the mind and heart until cries of mercy appear in the form of tears.

Tears? What do I know of about tears? Enough to know that when the dreadful pride clogs and stops the flow with refusal, denial, and numbing self-medicating, they fester within and flood the soul until it drowns in painful sorrow in some dreary, dismal despair. Sitting on a cracked headstone in a forgotten cemetery along Witchwood among the cold wet damp leaves of depressing November is just a distant memory now. I am down here in the summer night alongside the muddy banks of the Devils Creek, no wildflowers, just sticker bushes and poison ivy among the choking vines of parasitic poison oak and overgrown brush. I always thought I would find my lost love out here like the twisting end of the Witchwood stories, how she would ease my pain and explain to me that not only have I already died and was living in a state of limbo in denial…or was it a state of mercy created for me by sympathetic weeping angels with golden hearts? Whatever the ulterior motives, alternative worlds, fake planes, and deceiving dimensions are all created to ease the pain in a slow merciful way. In different realms of purgatory in higher and lower plateaus, I am given the advance evolution of learning and accepting the outcomes from my own thoughtless insensitive actions, taking the spiritually mature steps of growth from putting no blame on anyone else for my own cruel actions and words.

In perfect example for those poor souls who may not completely follow the whole purpose of Hela's Hellenism of the ancients Helheim, or for those who may not completely understand purgatory, go to your pipe collection, grab your favorite most expensive water pipe, bong, percolator, or hookah and throw it hard on the floor to shatter it like a "Born Too Late" old school, old spirit, brokenhearted, hopeless romantic considered a blind fool by today's tough old-world standards. Look at the pieces on the floor and tell the shattered pieces sorry, and for those more timid nonsmoking stoners, replace the bong with a china plate with the same scenario. Look down at the broken pieces and say sorry and realize then that in the spirit of old-school tough love, sorry doesn't cut it, meaning, sorry is just a word that holds not as much magic as people believe, even the most sincerest apologies may only be glue to the cracks that will never go away, but no word will make the bong or plate back to its original state. So in the foggy damp swamps of Hela's Helheim or the enchanting matrix illusions of purgatory is the painful lesson one must learn for being inconsiderate and uncompassionate to their fellow human beings, realizing the imperfections of an imperfect existence in an imperfect world and facing the pain to learn from those lessons. With all that being beyond the simplicity of casual mentioning and described in a "spell it out for you, paint a picture for you" is this: those were all the possibilities through teardrops and lonely longing answered with the kind of mercy that only comes in unspoken truth and empathy.

This is not about Witchwood Forest anymore; this is about Devils Creek and its dark magnetic undertow that calls those lost souls of Hela's foggy Helheim, just like the creeping fog that came out of the bowels of the belly of the beast deep within the dark heart of those haunted woods in them and they. The Black Mass Sabbath of secret covens drew down the moon in their dark robes and chants with the black goat sacrifice tied in the middle of the giant pentagram. Now we are getting closer to the real Devils Creek and closer and closer to not just one lost love like before when I wandered the forgotten weathered cemeteries of the ravages of time's pet weeds, moss, and rolling bones that swirl around the undertow of those deep murky, muddy waters with the fat dirty mud cats and numerous skulls that nature claims into the bosom of Mothers Nature's pagan elementals. No, no, no...that was the heartache of an obsessed broken heart and the despair of a fixated pain from the longing of a lost love, the missing of her smile, the sound of her laugh, the tones of whispering dreams stained with the nightmare of something taken and never to be replaced. Here along the muddy winding, twisting banks of old Devils Creek is the kind of bitterness of many lost loves and all the selfish reasons of lust that blinds the heart of love. Why? Why would someone choose the selfish simplicity of lust over the selfless power of love? For the gratifying instant relief of pleasure over the blood, sweat, and tears of time and patience of emotional hang-ups of the "Oh what tangled webs we weave."

Oh my dear faithful readers who have followed me long enough to this point that not only that we can chuckle to ourselves with a dark sense of humor that we are literally on the same page," but you love me as I do you because we the rare breed are all cut from the same cloth. Devils Creek is not what is above the menacing current of this dark haunted, hellish place, like the witch lines above giving enough electric residual to not only draw in spirits but keep those ones around. The old ley lines give them the power to be heard by the right ears and seen by the right eyes and scare the living shit out of those who are equally afraid of their own gifts of seeing and hearing them in the first place. Me, you may have might've wondered, yet I will never confess that I may already be dead and if I'm alive or dead, in purgatory, Helheim, or hell. Or maybe I am an innocent confused kid trapped in a man's body and bound by dementia. Nonetheless, walk among these whispering spirits without fear, even the grim reaper behind my shoulder patiently waits with a perched raven on his blade, and the hounds of hell relaxing at his feet know to keep a respectful distance from me, for just as almost all typical stories of death, the old reaper always has to wait for the soul he must escort to "the beyond' in which he came from. To help open and direct the eyes of the soul, he must collect until they see what he or she is meant to see first, and down here in Devils Creek, there were a few lost loves who had some things to say, things to say in ancient, ageless ways, things whispered from beyond, things spoken from beyond the grave. Messages from other realms, so bittersweet the melody of unspoken and unsung curses of love and hate, left dormant, stagnant, patiently for debate, the kind of debate that requires no response just the last two cents in the old rusty bucket, a penny for your thoughts.

Disgruntled grudges from angry judges are left in annoying smudges, reminding the weight of an obsessed fixation that never budges, just lingers, and looms like intricate silk designs marking the deadly bull's-eye on the webs from every stoned banana spider in the infested weeds from a forty-foot radius. Sweet venomous summer nights, wet weeds in humid dew drops, I tumble backward from careless steps head over heels down the embankment to the muddy banks of Devils Creek to cast my tear-filled eyes up the hill I just carelessly toppled down to catch the sight in the pale moonlight as

I hear the voices of beckoning sirens and banshees seductively and teasingly call my name, "Oh, Danny." Silent forests are filled with chirping crickets and croaking frogs. "Oh, sweet Daniel," they say as I scan the smashed weeds I left in the wake of my fall. My eyes readjust to the lunar moonlight glow to focus on just *exactly* what kind of weeds or brush I stumbled backwards down. The devil's harvest, the killer weed with the roots from hell, sweet-smelling Mary Jane fills my nostrils as my pupils let in more of the glowing moon light in shocking excitement. My vision is clouded with a hazy dark green trail of smashed overgrown marijuana plants surrounded by the towering untouched hundreds more that grew down the embankment to root strong where the water was.

Oh, the mighty Valkyries clear the way for the curious watching goddesses following my every move peering from behind the old oaks and maples. The divine, interested in the dark places only a curious goddess would dare to tread, is just as interested in my reaction to the same I hold in the familiar voices that call my name. "Daniel," a soft beckoning female's voice says again in a teasing manner. Even the goddess Freya hears them, which draws her just a little farther from her hiding place. I ignore goddess Freya acting as if I am unaware of her presence just as I keep her and the reaper both on both sides of my peripherals as I follow the familiar voices of lost loves toward the water's edge and the deadly still surface holding the broken moonlight image behind gently swaying tree limb tops. I slowly approach the banks to stare into the deceiving surface of the menacing dark moonlit waters, knowing damn well that what I suspect and fear will soon be confirmed for my brain and eyes to wrestle with. As I step up on the edge of the bank and stare into the moonlit surface a couple feet beneath my dark shadow, I see the Valkyries who guard Goddess Freya first come into view as they walk behind me, feeling their presence as Freya soon follows into view, all equally curious to catch a glimpse of what the water's reflection is about to reveal, all but death himself who by action of uninterest, content staying in the shadows, suggests he already knows what lost forgotten souls, angels, and goddesses all shyly and cautiously scramble to see, the dark sirens and banshees of past broken hearts. As I slowly step closer to the menacing currents of Devils Creek's edge, I see her, her reflection, but so much more. This isn't just the shimmering outer reflection of the ghost of a lost love unseen over my shoulder but her clearly smiling with a haunting eye contact of telepathic unspoken words in a penetrating gaze as well. These are the reflections of all the lost loves in the murky cold depths of Devils Creek, all staring up at me with no need for voices, just the piercing eyes with the unspoken words "Come to us." Even goddesses and dark banshees back up behind me as if they were looking at deadly quicksand. The allure of their sincerest, most sorrowful gazes locked into my own eyes have me paralyzed with a mix of regret and curiosity. These are not wistful, tearful reflections of heartbroken regret of once beautiful smiling angels full of life. These were resentful, unforgiving stares of guilt waiting to lock their hypnotizing eyes onto mine in vengeful entrapment from beyond the murky currents of the deep muddy Devils Creek, and even as Sirens and Banshees of the darkest hours back away in realization of what they know all too well, I foolishly kneel down at the water's edge to make sense of what I am seeing that even the most nocturnal sinister tricksters have already figured out and left. The only two supernatural beings that have chosen to stay in my shadows, watching in pity from a safe distance, are the beautiful compassionate goddess Freya and the grim reaper even farther back in the misty fog. These reflections of all the women I was given a chance to love but arrogantly or foolishly or blindly passed up by being doomed to be too simple-minded and too slow to catch on, have all come to show the faces of disappointment and heartbreak that I unknowingly and unintentionally caused by some dark malevolent grudge, equivalent to the same grudges I held on them for being so arrogant to believe that it is always the men who have to make the first move—the lonely curse to all the shy, the slow, the dreamers, and the timid.

The very she devil succubus still haunts and taunts from underneath the surface of devils creek, to rub it in the kindred soft innocent hearts of all the assholes they fucked while us good guys stayed up alone and depressed with insomnia. Although at one point they may have all been crushes and objects of fantasy and admiration, make no mistake as to what they were really, what all of us kindhearted "slow" fools took longer to see, to see them for what they truly were—the hideous, heartless sirens from the deep here to rub it in the faces of all the gentlemen once more, the false guilt, the self-esteem-crushing, relentless, merciless hatred for not making the first move. The punishment for carrying a lifelong ego-crushing self-esteem-destroying dark cloud of lingering regret? No apologies, no explanations, just the hellish show of watching all our angels become whores and fuck everyone but us and then just as always as how the story always goes.

In the unfair, cruel, hateful lesson and spirit of "nice guys finish last," I realize that it is not a reflection of my heavy-hearted regrets in the murky surface, but the illusion for what it really is.... Dragging the waters for the most painful lesson to be realized, something left behind to painfully remember in the depths of the dangerous undertow, that nothing was my fault, nothing was any of the good guy's fault; it was all just meant to be carelessly and hatefully believed to be thought it was our fault, when in all reality, it was their guilt. They were not reflections; they were the hideous sirens underneath the deceiving pretty smiles and made-up dolled-up faces of mirages and illusions wrung out of every drop of nine lives and borrowed time put out on display with a heartless pride of the illusions and the discarding of the fragile emotion that makes us all human and teeters on the edge of what turns that humanity into selfish, greedy monsters with the fake artificial masks of reputation. Reputation? A shield of self-made alter ego to make the frightened fragile person underneath feel a false sense of security. Masks of the sirens, beautiful on the outside but hideous on the inside—masks to pull me into the murky brutal rolling undertows to add to their collections of decayed bones of all the men they've eaten alive, the men who weren't afraid to make the first move, the men who were not afraid to say the first corny one liner, their bones rolling up against the rotting logs and rocks along the catfish while the sirens tried to allure me in closer. Once I realized the brutal truth that had eluded me my whole life, I gasped a deep breath of disgust and shock, followed by a deep exhale of a sigh of relief. It seems I wasted many tears and years crying over the wrong women. The she demons disguised as angels, ravenous man-eating succubi in human form, are nothing more but bottom-feeding bloodthirsty tricksters waiting with the muddy catfish and snapping turtles to claim what they never could have—a soul, a heart, and a conscience. Down here in the dismal, dreary, dark midnight weeds, I would recall all the lonely times I would sit alone talking to myself, attempting to do what all the selfish, greedy she devil succubi could never do—comfort me with warm words of reassuring positivity and strength to experience what was under the murky undertow, revealing the borrowed time of that has kept me here for endless despair. Never was there an escape or some elaborate getaway, it was simply just a taste of a life I never knew. The more I got to experience the ugly, vulgar underbelly of the tough old world's undertow that lurked and lingered beneath the surface, the more I embraced my desperate delusional depression of my loner lifestyle of a lunatic lost. These realizations pushed the grim reaper further from my view and back into his own personal path into the thick pitch-black brush of the thick wild foggy forests that claimed him just as much as he claimed and embraced it, as much as it did the same for him, some dark eternal embrace, a calling and a claiming of something that was just as much as part of the night as the hazy ancient misty moon the wolves cried out too as the creatures not of this world danced with the fellow lost spirits from beyond.

Down here, under the old hellish bridge of Devils Creek, covered in spray-painted graffiti of satanic symbols and rituals that only a trained eye could make sense of from the beer-stenched back seat of weed-smoking heavy metal. A ghost of my former self in a shell of what was once me is long gone through ageless, lost, and lonely nights, somewhere up there in beer can-littered overgrown ditches and black wax melted guard rails of satanic mass. Waiting in the cool summer breeze beyond the howls of the lunatic predator, riding high above the calling sirens and the screams of the banshees are the gentle angels long passed away into ghosts of the ceremony. Somehow, somewhere I was stuck in the middle of beautiful, enchanting life and decadent decaying death with the sympathies and empathetic compassions of goddess Freya always several steps ahead in the distance making careful way in unstopped cautionary trailblazing steps ahead accompanied by her personal obedient angels, and far behind lagging, lurking, and creeping in the misty, foggy dark shadows was death trailing behind attentively with his own obedient faithful flocks of watchful ravens. I was neither in the present world of the living as most of us know it, nor was I in the realm of the spirit world either, somewhere in between where war-seasoned battle-braved Valkyries brushed aside the obstacles of Helheim, for Hela's own legendary all-seeing piercing eyes herself catch an admiring interested glimpse, already catching her intriguing attention of not only escaping the beckoning sirens' murky death trap from Devils Creek's dark undertow but for seeing them for what they were (harpies of the damned).

Somewhere were some would call heaven and hell and what the more ancients would refer to as Valhalla and Helheim was what we all could agree as an endless time known as purgatory, a place in between where one must spiritually earn their stripes in moral awakening. It is a spiritual realm for the brave and the cowardly, the strong and the weak, the blunt and outspoken, and the shy and timid to test the enchanting magical limits and edges of the mind, spirit, and heart. Once I remember so long ago through the shining flaming eye of the sun, on lost warm summer days years ago, before there was more than just ten channels on television. Video games and cell phones killed the what was then social common ground of people actually leaving their homes and actually doing things in the great outdoors. I recall these things in fond recollection with you because these were the warm bright summer days when Devils Creek was frequently visited and occupied by free-spirited people, some strange and weird, some outgoing and friendly, but all shared the common thread of the love of the shady muddy banks of Devils Creek, with its shimmering radiant sun dancing across its own reflection in bright glimmers on fresh humid air. Oh, the sweet smell of the summer air with the array of combinations of flowers and weeds. The weed was a common code for the beer drinking anglers that carried their coolers of beer to wash down the exhales of marijuana joints or doobies. Even the stoner lingo and slangs are so much different now than back in those days under the sun.

I glance now around me in the dark lonely night listening to the crickets chirping over the whispering spirits of those very people, gone but not forgotten. I bring you back to the early days of this old creek for a very important lesson, a meaningful purpose for some food for thought. After all, if I am to share with you the stories of my haunted stomping grounds and the legendary repetition that grows in its name with each lost, lonely passing season, then it is seemingly even more fitting that I take you back to small glimpses of forgotten innocent memories of times and places, the faces of happy souls who eventually never come back. Just to my left in the eerie pale moonlight I stare, and then I turn my head to the right to make the connection of sorrowful realizations that weigh heavily on a saddened heart that longs to hear the laughter of those once living ghosts of Devils Creek's happy histories and gloomy mysteries. To each side of me, just faintly visible under the summer moon, are the remnants of what used to be well-worn trails and clearings that never needed to be mowed or hacked away by machete. It was just a simpler time years ago that people actually got out and explored, venturing out to a calling heart, answering the need to be a part of this world, this earth, this forgotten nature that once held the loud chirps and cheerful songs of flocks of birds in the tree tops. Now birds are few, as so are the insects. No one notices these things because everyone stays in the air-conditioned homes playing with their cell phones that have somehow became less than just a material object but more as an appendage or detachable limb. No one, that is, as far as I can tell, yet I notice, and if anyone else does, it seems just a small passing thought in a shrug as they throw out their cigarettes and beer bottles out the windows as they drive over Devils Creek's bridge.

Once upon a fading memory before this was even called Devils Creek, it was simply called Grantfork Creek, or more properly Silver Creek, named so because it flowed in or, judging by the fast-moving current, out of the town's infamous Silver Lake with its dangerous notorious undertows. Of course, if you were to look down into its sinister waters, there was nothing silver at all about its dark chocolate-colored muddy waters. Now in this lonely refuge of random repetition of reflecting on reaping what we all sow to both sides of me are overgrown brush, sticker bushes, tangled vines of clinging burrs and poison oak, ivy, and sumac of what was once well-worn trails so long ago. Only to my trained eyes do I even know the faint difference that reveals what was once there and will never be again. My heart is heavy for humanity. Have we as a race reached our peak of happy, joyful existence? The celebration of every precious moment of enchanting minutes and seconds uncounted by math and adored and loved by magic? Oh, the magic…the enchanting magic, it's all still very much here, but our peak as a human race is dwindling downward in forgotten footsteps of loved ones walking hand in hand and separated in seclusion by an illusion of brainwashed material things distracting us from the beauty, the delusions and conspiracy theories numbing and desensitizing everyone's beautiful all-seeing premonitions of divine déjà vu.

With no more clues, we blind ourselves from the truth that cries out to deaf ears, waving its love-starved arms for the attention it is starving for in front of blind eyes texting conspiracies to uncaring, preoccupied people. All the trails to all the good fishing spots are overgrown and forgotten just like the unkempt graves and cemeteries up behind me in the wooded hills of Witchwood Forest. Old time black magic howls in the late night wind while the black cats and crazy foxes carefully circle silently within the high spider-infested weeds. Bleached bones of primitive prey hunted in heaping mounds of our ancestors' resting place, the cool summer night breeze kisses my face as the tears trickle down my cheeks. Old great earth with all your enchanting wonders and mysterious life trickling away like oil and paint polluting the Devils Creek, a place where no fish caught would be fit to be eaten and a place I pray timeless magic will someday mend and heal what's true and real out here in solitude while the town folk laugh away miles into town in their bars and emission-flunking cars with cell phones in hand. The lonely girl I could've saved if only I could've met her and had some deep meaningful heartfelt conversation tries to cross the street but almost gets run over by some passing texter. All the cool safe havens of hang-out friends are all gone and replaced by selfish, greedy, hateful fiends ready to make her "cool" by social gang raping and passing her around. Our inner light is being stamped out before it can even shimmer a faint spark and grow into a flame. The wings of the butterflies are being picked off before they can spread to the skies and proudly show their true magnificent colors.

I sit here in the dark in the quiet muddy banks of Devils Creek picking the weeds while black moths flutter and swarm around me. I occasionally pick up a small muddy rock and toss it into the moon's reflection to watch it ripple. There is one more beautiful lady out there I will never save, so chin up and be brave, wipe the dirt from your face, because this lonely place is the tears of Mother Nature as she claims back her earth in front of dazed days of delirious delusion. I walked the old railroad tracks to the city alone through miles of secluded sticks that even the bravest fear to tread, dismissing their fears by names and labels like Bum Fuck Egypt, but it was the crossroads where I heard his footsteps, and it was my bleeding heart worn so proudly on my sleeve that brought me a deal I never asked for but was almost impossible to pass up. The timeless eyes rotting down here in the last final dusk, down here in the endless night to watch humans wipe each other off the face of the earth and walk with the angels who will see and understand things that I will never see or understand, to understand Witchwood Forest's lonely regrets, to feel the dreamlike enchantment of Devils Creek's spell, to face *them* and *they* in ancient ageless reincarnations. Only the hearts of old souls and shooting stars could ever brave the torment, then one night, one of so many endless countless lonely nights, we all must stop and look behind us to not only wait for what follows to finally catch up but to face what none of us can outrun—sweet, sorrowful fate, with its bittersweet, dreadful denial of destiny.

Wait for what follows to catch up and face your demons. Look into the eyes of what may have the answers to what torments you so deeply, for in the spirit of we fear what we don't understand, sometimes to prevent from ever reaching that frightening task that everyone dreads, it is easier to keep the fear alive by covering it with unreachable mountains of lies to bury it under. Old wise tales, myths, to keep the fear alive, so in the spirit of misery loves company, I will wait for death to scout the summer fog to find me approachable by the stalking hellhounds hidden in the fog and the legendary infamous devil who waits for me to sense his presence and present a presentable open invitation of patient waiting instead of fearful fleeing, persistent pursuing of personal and painful perception, an anxiously anticipated inception that fearless never experience rejection, and so it follows, a steady pace in a losing race. The turtle and the rabbit, one frantically runs for its life with panic-filled exhaustion and the other keeps a slow steady pace, with wise all-seeing caution, never seen or out of place, dark sinister eyes that can read any emotionless face.

The things that follow and the time they borrow, the lunar glow of the moonlight shine, the truest most mysterious souls living on borrowed time. And so beyond the lonely whispering twisted branches of the dancing treetops of Witchwood dark haunted woods, far past the ominous deep sticks of the infamous ley-line possessed trees, shines just above the top tree lines were the midnight stars and slowly moving moon that creeps and glides across the universe night sky like some cosmic snail sneaking away in a silent escape from the despair and pain is the glow of a city just a few miles away. It is a city that has rejected and forgotten me and then forgot its insensitive, heartless shunning, so the guilt of being a "perfect" gossiping Christian won't show through the heavy makeup in the reflection of their mirrors reminding them that none of them cares. The glow over the treetops as the night breeze blows just a little hard enough to create a small chill reminds me I am alone and do not belong, so silent out here away from the loud bars and local bands playing over the rich drunk socialites and their judging cliques.

Out here in the foggy darkness and dew-dropped weeds, I am alone if I choose to be like them out there in the city and pretend to not acknowledge the company of those unworldly mythological creatures who never stopped following me because I was cut from the same cloth as their very condemned existence. They, like me, are forgotten in a fearful denial. Down the slopes of the ancient ley lines, the natives hundreds of years before that town was ever built knew of and walked cautiously with respect, as the tree filled slopes up top never had the endless decayed headstones from forgotten time, down the trails that lead down here in Devils Creek where I've been sitting here with the forgotten and shunned things people deny their existence keeping me company in dismal sorrow. I never truly know what offered me more immediate comfort in the selfish forms of instant gratification on those cold lonely mornings. I curled up my dirty blankets in with lonely despair whispering sweet nothings in my empty ears or the drugs coursing through my veins, the warm rush as it hits the base of my skull, dispersing some mystic magical venom to creep through all my veins and gently cast the silent sight of the spider's many eyes spinning her web, wounding weird and wild weeping wishes away from wondering minds and the fearful dread of what it is to find and unwind borrowed deadly dreams distantly damaging some damnation that follows far behind. The lonely deep observation from within, a deep inner reflecting of past lives has rekindled the flames of demonic family curses of dark haunting spells on infestations and incantations of invocations of *them* and *they*. The spell of conception and perception control the delusions and illusions of an altered reality with a creative disease of an infected imagination. The tormentors and parasitic followers of old-time black magic spells slowly creep in lumbering stalking, the fear of those who follow and steal away tomorrow.

Stolen suns, replaced with dreary rainy days of depressing gloom and doom, force me and you to sleep these dark, dismal misery away so they have you wide awake all night. The things within those dark days always follow, and when they catch up, they visually hide among you staying close by in the shadows and fog in the dark stormy raindrops whispering insecurities of low self-esteem and apathy as they fester with you and within you in your lonely melancholy to wait and burn away all your sanity in relentless cruel torture, merciless madness going insane, begging for compassion in mental anguish and physical pain until the ones who control the ones who follow finally appear to take you once and for all, away from the torment with the ultimate sacrifice of personal vanity and pride. Not the retreat, not the escape, not the chase, or the denial of fate but the ancient and ageless destiny that all the cursed and damned must face, the *defeat* and *not* the retreat. Accept that you can run but can't hide, for how can you hide from the things that can dwell within and enter inside? Possess your thoughts and speech? Witchwood Forrest and

Devils Creek, the ancient past lives of the eternal torment of *them* and *they*. Till you accept the defeat to the point of shedding all fear and finally stop running and stand and wait for *them* to draw near. Face your sins, rather give into them, your vanity and pride, your sloth and your lies and so much more, to shut the door of sunny days to never reopen it again. In the spirit of "if you cannot beat them, join them," you give *them* and all hell that has followed permission to take you, have you, own you, possess you, and make you their ungodly monstrous pet, immortal, undead. To flush all the pain of the torment of the leagues of relentless parasites away and replace it with eternal infinite darkness with no escape, you become them, as what I become, fading Sorrow, an endless night. Those who may be forced to face the unfair hands we've been dealt with must first accept the simple rule of thumb in the hard-to-face brutal truth of ignored and overlooked facts—nothing in this life or the next is ever fair, and it's even harder to find those in the endless seas of lost souls who even care.

What unseen angel hands would have the painful overbearing empathy and heart-wrenching sympathy to step into this lonely plane of existence and offer a caring hand to hold while the other hand points in brave and courageous direction of affection like a strong and sturdy lighthouse under the dark morning stars' misty fog? Symphony of empathy falls on deaf ears and blind eyes under shimmering stars in misty morning dense dark skies. There is no leading, guiding angels, just me alone drowning in hateful lies, the incoherent ramblings of the lost and insane trying to escape death and cheat all the pain. I look up to the only lonely single bridge that crosses over Devils Creek and recall the late setting dawn's summer sun in lonely beauty that desperately needed to be shared with another living human being, but alone in the beauty of the setting sun in a faraway beautiful place, golden brown fields of prairie littered with wildflowers and butterflies that even every animal from wolves to horses would run through in joyful love of living. There in the distance are the ones I love the most; the ones I miss and adore in lost precious time that can never be retrieved all say the unspoken yet very clearly heard words that we all sometimes have a hard time saying—don't go. The heart-wrenching words of irretrievable pleas of choked back tears in lonely sunsets—don't leave. All those who long for companionship, for those who dearly miss those so close to their heart instead feel an overwhelming tremendous grief that never leaves.

Down here under this bridge on old Devils Creek, struggling and suffering through isolation, the important lessons in life, the other side of loss and despair, is longing to be with someone who cares. Those who ever said that time does not wait on no one has never experienced the private hell of ghostly purgatory in the still midnight fog. The natives speak of a spirit world in every religion, belief, race, and country all share some version of these inner dimensions of time and space of alternate worlds, universes, and endless worlds. The dark empty vacuum of nothingness of being born back into this world without a normal-thinking brain, just the confused eyes of shock and bewilderment encased and suppressed in deep lost memories hidden and locked away in the old corn asylums of abandoned farms far out in the country. Some old barn owl sits up in the hay stable quietly watching as a lost frightened child wanders alone, scared and alone. As I searched the empty void in my confused, lost mind of some kind of catatonic autistic brain-dead existence that was somehow forced on me to forget some kind of dreadful action, I may have accidentally witnessed and been brainwashed or hypnotized to forget and then thrown out into the tough old world with the hungry wolves hoping that I would be devoured, taking the suppressed memories forever with me. Spoon-feeding the catatonic child lost in a state of shock, the swirling magnetic photographic lenses of forever tripped-out eyes, a silent mute, lost in life as a deaf, dumb, and blind walking observer somehow tape-records and films this painful existence in this loveless life to report back to God after my death.

Sometimes when God would speak to me through God winks and strangers would talk in a weird language only I knew, they would sometimes help me perceive it as a present-time spy for God. I am one of God's scared and confused lost sinners, scared and alone, frightened and missing home, kicked around in the cold wet streets alone, hungry and scared. I long for the warmth of love, missing my family but left to wander the empty streets in the rain like that "People are Strange" song by the band called The Doors and remembering how easily I could relate to Jim Morrison, a fellow Sagittarius and also a fellow lost soul. The dark rain came with the loud thunderstorms, with that rare kind of freak thunder that didn't just boom and rumble with a quick loud short boom that made most people jump, no, no, not this thunder. This was the kind of thunder that frightened even the saints and would make even heroes and holy men pull the covers over their eyes as the thunder would rumble on in long growling, rumbling of Thor's Hammer as if the gods were bowling on giant moon-sized bowling balls slowly rolling down the halls of Valhalla until they finally struck the planets aligned like bowling pins with the loud claps of lightning bolts. Like Odin's stomach was growling for more feasting and drinking, the freakishly long drawn-out thunder growled the kind of doom that would send only the maddest berserkers to run with the hunting wolves in the pitch-black night.

My eyes have stared into those berserk eyes until they eventually became the photographic-style lenses of memories and emotions lost and forgotten to me but recorded and documented for the observation of God. To watch one of his innocent brain-dead children, lost, scared, and heartbroken, wandering lonely adventures through his tear-filled eyes. Just like that song "Hollywood Nights" by Bob Seeger, in that infamous line, "He looked at all those bright lights as they shined over LA, he knew right away, he was too far from home"—that line touched that lost, scared, lonely child within that everyone could see in me but me. I remember playing alongside the creek beds and shores of the local farm ponds, catching frogs and snakes. Being born from a conscious state of mind from previous lifetimes confused me at an early age, for as I turned from a child to a kid in his twenties, then his thirties, then eventually his midforties, yet I still feel like that very same confused ancient Egyptian pharaoh royal child trapped in a confused aging body riddled in heartbreaking emotional pain and the excruciating, painful degenerative spinal disease that hurt so bad that death would become an obsessing thought as a release for the pain. It was a hellish roller coaster of being too poor to stay stocked in the blessed illegal street drugs that I learned to love so dearly, my sweet, sweet heroin. How I worshipped it enough of countless many years that the creeping thought in the back of my mind that only at first would come and go like a nightmare, would creep up as a returning nightmare in reality form, that always ever-present, lingering thought looming over all other thoughts in the back of my mind.

The painful state always comes back to haunt me, but after a while it eventually comes so many countless times with the worst zombie-inducing immobilizing, excruciating pain that even when I would finally always find a way to chase it away once more by the euphoric nirvana of chasing all the pain and anxiety away that I would convince this stalking hellhound that always was close behind that it was just a nightmare and he would never come back.... And to kill that hellhound called "Dope-Sick" by the soothing mercy of those magical words "get right" or "get well" or "get my fix" would eventually linger there in the back of the mind in the most perfect painless escapes, escaping from the breathless panting of anxiety and panic attacks, escaping from the excruciating pain of spinal-desecrating arthritis, escaping from my fears and phobias of socializing with those who do not understand me, escaping all my other poor health problems. But the lingering looming hellhound called dope sick has hurt me so many times, bringing with it all those things I escape in a stronger concentrated dose that eventually even escaping it would not be able to kill the hellish nightmare of reality's factual promise that "You can run, but you cannot hide." Eventually that old snarling, foaming-at-the-mouth rabies-infested dope-sick hellhound will be there waiting with undying patience waiting when all the dear sweet medicine runs out. The escape from the mental and physical and emotional pain always costs the price of having to spend the unwanted time with the hellhound.

This horrific haunting tale of this relentless stalking hellhound always finds me in the muddy muck of the swampy banks of Devils Creek to smother me and drown me in the very excruciating pain I run from. That old excruciating unbearable pain always eventually comes creeping up from behind to remind me what kind of tormenting pain was stalking and creeping around me in the marshy, swampy lowland banks of this old Devils Creek, down here under this bridge while death and his hellhounds mill around in the darkness patiently abiding the time to feast on my pain as I am forced to stare into the madness of piercing red eyes of rabies-infested muddy hounds of hell, dripping the foam from their mouths as the growls contain a hissing backward old tongue language of Latin spells of misery and woe. Eventually there is the repetitious pain that everyone in this world do their best to avoid, the lingering, creeping eternal void, the fog of society's worldwide paranoia, the mere very thought that stresses out all mortal souls make us all intensely panicky and annoyed. Many poor lost souls with these feelings forced the begging mercy of making these unfortunate tormented souls commit suicide or slip into a painful psychosis of lonely heartbreaking madness that creates unseen multiple personalities walk silently beside the manifesting insane apparitions of the depressing gut-wrenching heartache from deep inside. I was born into a numb autistic, painful, lonely state of existence and felt the pain of life's silent depressing resistance, and the one medicine that I found that cures me from all the soul-crushing persistence of held back choked-down tears that drown my heart in my state of mind that has dragged me down into a silent solitude of being hard to read and being so distant. My mind-torturing insane isolation of madness brewed and stewed in long bouts of despair, starving for just one understanding soul that still loves and is not afraid to care. I often wonder when I wander down here with all the lost forgotten world somewhere up here on that bridge, speeding over to face the night with a perfect world in front of them and all the right friends and places to go and things to do.

As I peer up at the hovering yellowish and greenish lunar glow of the cratered moon through the rustling summer night treetops of shaking leaves, whispering magical pagan secrets in the twisted forest surrounding me, my mind drifts to the dream we all wish we had, that special time we all only seemingly so briefly felt truly alive, amazed, and dazed by all the magical wonder and beauty of life around us. The magic in the stars up high on a moonlight midnight drive with the summer in breeze in my hair… Recall…if at all? Was I ever truly alive? Or did I die, as the angels wept for the soul of an innocent child never being able to really live a life that was sadly and tragically cut short long before the growth peek of my prime? The angels wept along with the grieving ones who loved me, or was it us? Were you there too? I think we all were at this point in our life where we all recollect a time in our lives when we realize that the best has passed us by, and all we are, all any of us are or any of us are doing is just hanging on, waking up with the haunted house window shades drawn closed where another day above ground is a blessing and truly better than the alternative. When we died as young children, the angels wept along with our maker and makers, our siblings and parents, and relatives on permanent vacation, and we weep ourselves for warmth and salvation in a cold cruel world that turned out the lights. So…this is where I take you where I am at, down here in Devils Creek in a small place among many others where I felt so alive, amazed, and enchanted and connected in a world that rejected me for being so different and not the same.

Nothing has changed while we all go insane, in our invisible chains that distract us all from the pain. The angels created a world where I can live out a life in a dream as a ghost that does not realize that I met my demise so many, many moons ago. All the blessed details of beautiful memories beg all of us as human beings to really believe that there is so much more out there than just this life down here in the swampy muddy banks of Devils Creek. I stare up at the moon through the treetops as the world around me moves on, and as life goes on till pain and age consumes us, my surroundings fade away, and I'm back in the early seventies in an old sixties Chevy pickup truck, with the headlights piercing through the thick bunches of sloppy clumsy flying insects of the night. Moths, dragonflies, gnats, and fireflies all dive-bomb into the grill of the truck until the grill and front hood and windshield are smeared with hundreds of dead bugs. If you are still following me, then ask yourself…where did all the bugs go? Down south in a Florida dumpster where jumbo giant flying cockroaches wait their turn to take back the earth? What happened to all the fuzzy caterpillars, wooly worms, and all the hundreds of spiderwebs in every nook and cranny, crack and corner?

Something is amidst, and if you can figure out just exactly what is wrong with the world around you, then maybe you will finally figure out all those nagging, annoying questions that haunt and taunt you. Like, for example, if you're still alive and living? Or are you just waiting your turn to die? The headlights are still filled with moshing bugs and clumsy flying insects slam dancing in the summer night air, as the backdrop soundtrack fills my ears with the mixed symphony of a combination of frogs and crickets and night-crawling critters singing into the still of the night accompanied by the smell of summertime nighttime weeds and wildflowers and the sweet smell of rich fresh dirt. My heart beats to the rhythms of the backbeat sounds of the sacred night when I realize I'm not driving this wide old rusty Chevrolet truck. The wide single bench in the single cab, as the loud rusty broken muffler almost sounds like old cherry bombs, I realize that I'm in the middle with someone sitting on both sides of me, but the truck is so old and wide that there is plenty of room between me and the two guys sitting next to me. The guy to my right is my son and the guy driving is my dad. We are all the same age, all three of us are somehow unexplainably and mysteriously eighteen. Good old classic rock is playing on the eight-track player, as the crickets and frogs fill our ears with chirps and croaks. Bullfrogs and owls chime in as the old Chevrolet cruises down the old blacktop country road. I do not have to ask either one where we are going, because we all happily and contently already know. We are going to hear the soundtrack of the night in James Whites's Old Ripley fishing pond. We are all young and healthy, in no pain and in the right weight. This is why there was so much room on both sides of me. We are all only a buck seventy-five, buck eighty in perfect health, all in our prime. As approaching headlights creep up slowly behind us, catching up to our speed, I catch a reflection of my eyes in the windshield and then a quick flash of my face as the car behind begins to pass.

Looking at myself for that split second revealed what I already knew, I was eighteen again, and the world was a heart-pounding mysterious wonder of awe and enchantment. As I look to my left as the old (one of Grampa's cars) pass by, I see my two grampas, and they, too, are young, free, and proud. In the back seat are three cousins all the same age. My grandfathers lead the way, and after a few miles of all of us following them as we pass a joint and drink some cold old-fashioned peel-top beers, my grandfathers turn on a left turn signal and pull into a weedy overgrown dirt road as we hear all the sticker bushes and branches scratch and scrape the bottom and sides of the slow rumbling truck, headlights still filled with clumsy frantic bugs. The closer we get to the old fishing pond, the louder the crickets and frogs get. We can hear the old bass hum of the bullfrogs and the rattling of fishing poles and tackle boxes along with old aluminum folding chairs that slide up and down the rusty bed of the Chevy. There is a multiverse and a number of portholes to enter and leave inner dimensional beings have seen, somewhere in between reality and a dream. Across the bullfrog pond is a moving walking thing, an inner dimensional sasquatch in backwoods with a reefer in Danny boy and Mick's moonlight plants.

Somewhere along them old dirt roads with a tree line on one side and miles of endless cornfields hides this reefer-smoking bigfoot, or so it appears, as an inside joke, but maybe more realistically a marijuana plant watchdog, an illegally homegrown watch bigfoot. Oh, unholy skunk ape, for reefer-stealing rednecks, there is no freaking escape. Me and my son giggle and laugh as we reminisce those wild summer nights, much like this strange magical one of generation of siblings, father and sons, grandpas, cousins. The rearview mirror keeps collecting old-timey dim headlights as they sloppily swerve side to side under the cool summer night air as Neil Young plays his raw tin-pan blues fuse of psychedelic classic rock over the cracked speakers—"hello, cowgirl in the sand, passing joints in hand." The dirt roads all gather, slowing down classic cars, switching headlights to yellow glowing parking lights. One by one they all pull off into the weeds off the old dirt road. The smell of summertime soil and wild weeds fill our nostrils while the sound of nature's nocturnal symphony blends in with the summer night smell like a beautiful, enchanting midnight spell of amazing wonder. The recipe for lost reality wept and slept then is swept away under the covers of a neatly made bed someplace far from the wild nature of midnight mayhem magically made to marvel in maniacal madness. The moon moves mysteriously as I hear the familiar voice of my grampa Donald, my dad's dad, looking no older than twenty-one. "Daniel," he calls out my name with a smile. Is it really him? He's been gone for so many years, and here he is right before me in his prime, in perfect time, under the moonshine. Standing in line are all my uncles and cousins, all the same age. Even my nephews are here, River, Kayne, and Domenico all holding their fishing poles and tackle boxes. "Grampa, is that really you?" I ask as I step in closer and feel the group of family all surround me from behind as we all step in closer together. "Yes, I hope so, Daniel," Grampa replies. "At least it feels like me," he adds.

"Is any of this real?" My uncle Lloyd asks, as my son Mickey and my nephews all laugh, which triggered a domino effect of a laughing avalanche. My dad walks to an old upside-down Jon boat in the weeds and asks my uncle David and my cousin David to flip it over and scan for spiderwebs, revealing a few squatting bullfrogs using the boat as shelter. Uncle Donald steps up from my right and says, "This is just like the good old Kaskaskia River days, huh, Daniel?" I look around and see that Uncle Donald looks to be at the age of twenty-one, maybe twenty-two. I am here in a promised chain of life, each one of my family members, uncles, grampas, cousins, all a separate link of many links.

Down here in the doom and gloom of the hollow, whispering wishes forgotten on lonely dusty high noons, the murky muddy undertow with snakes through this thick brush of Witchwood Forest's dark pagan eyes, how the old creek winds. The wind blows tonight; it howls and whistles through old broken branches that rustles hissing leaves, whispering strange curses that can't let me leave. The crickets and frogs remind me not to forget to breathe, because there is something amidst among a world that feels like a dream, a world you never even knew existed. Any time throughout your life, your mind refused to choose to accept and resisted. When you go, do people know? Do they miss you or even knew what was left behind? Just another world, some are hard to find, and if I mind and walk away, leaving my youthful family far behind in my wake, the sound of their conversations grow more and more muffled as they fade into the sounds of the night. Exploring worlds within worlds, the elements of inner dimensional travel. We were all planned to be where we are at a certain point in time. My parents knew me years before I was born; they knew I was coming. When I came to this earth, this world, I felt like an old soul, a visitor.

Years ago, around my gramma's pond, my sisters and mother, all young and full of life, walk along the farm house looking for goose eggs. My cousins are all the same age as my aunts and mom. All hang out with my gramma baking pies in the kitchen. Where does time go—the age-old question that we all asked ourselves so many years ago, then eventually the same unanswered questions come creeping back during our midlife crisis to remind us once again all the frightening unknown things that come echoing through the eternal void of black hole space matter. The point is, was this all a dream? If so, what magical parts of our lives are intertwined forever with those we love, those we knew, those we only knew of, and those we never knew at all... Was there a young great-great-grampa there that night fishing with the ancient limbs of a swaying family tree creaking in the nighttime summer breeze? Was there a great-great-gramma and her grammas in the kitchen of that old farmhouse baking all-American apple pies? The magic of the cassette recorder is held in the tiny hands of my cousins Misty and Ada. They captured and caught my bewildered voice in the small black box and played it back to me as the geese waddled alongside the farm pond guarding the very eggs used to make the pies and cakes of the congregating women of the family tree clan. The leaves rustle high above my head in the age-old world of dingy futures and bright black-and-white pasts on old steel-bladed box fans blowing on us tiny children as we watched old-timey cartoons, sitting Indian style on the green carpets on the old huge wooden box television. The ghosts of time portals and space travel in glow in the dark humming and hovering floating spheres faster than any car or plane weaving in and out of the farmland.

Past-life memories somehow call me back out of this wondering dream down here in Devils Creek, where I remember fishing with my dad, uncle, and cousin. The old played-out roll of tape spins reruns of memories like a favorite show with no other alternatives and nowhere to go. It was the boondocks back in 1973 and 1975 that had us all grueling over climbing the metallic walls. My parents told me they remembered us climbing the walls with the bright lights shining through the windows, but what an odd thing to say. What an odd thing to remember as I recalled those strange years that my parents will not talk about anymore. A strange type of Alzheimer's has stricken the family but not the kind that you see the elderly have. This is the kind of Alzheimer's where memories have been erased yet day-to-day life is still perfectly functional. These are suppressed buried memories, with all the bridges to recollect those memories burned down. This is what it's like to have an erased memory Alzheimer's. The mind has no problem recognizing familiar faces, places, and things. It has no problem remembering directions or doing equations, for the most part the brain is perfectly normal and fine until some kind of smell or sight, vision or sound may trigger backwaters flowing like the muddy currents of Devils Creek. I am in a catatonic vegetable state of being forced to forget something that I cannot remember, Christmas lights on lonely roads on a cold and lonely December. There is something on the tip of my tongue that I cannot say, unable to place my trembling finger on it, no tomorrow without yesterday. Did I die all those years ago? And upon my death, did a reanimated reflection of deaths' rejection breathe life back into the vessel like a visionary projection? An alternate universe from the multiverse, a witch's spell from a dark pagan curse, down here under the bridge.

Over top drives a hearse, snakeskin dangles off the bridge's underbelly like flashbacks when it got worse. The echo doom of the planet moon that is not a planet at all, and the reflection of its tune, a tritone of raven's gloom, because the moon is too small. So the pagans would draw down the moon in ancient ceremony as UFOs would hover nearby and shooting stars over passing cars would be oblivious to the overhead sky. Two steps turn into twenty feet, and it's easy to move along the banks of Devils Creek, when bigfoot lurks along to creep up and greet. All this tongue-tied magic isn't as tragic as you may think, it's just helping you remember what would normally take a shrink. Psychiatrists and nurse practitioners did their best to string me along, but my memory is failing me; it gets weaker instead of strong. I watch the spinning stars drift around in full sessions in seasonal bliss. Lifetimes have been slowed down so the eyes no longer see this. Ancient are my ways as seconds are like days, generations of invitations watch me go as I stay. I'm in the words of evolving speech, simple thoughts that I can teach; telepathic extra sensory isn't hard for me to reach. There are decades in a blink, as constellations give out a wink way up high. Just look straight up, somewhere down here as I fill up my cup. Give out a cheers for lost forgotten years, drink to life, love, stars above, laughter, and tears.

There is a winding, twisting country road that drives out of town; it takes you past a cemetery on a hill that descends down. Just past Witchwood Forest and old woods filled with crows lay Devils Creek. Banks are steep, but the ley lines are low. The witch lines hold magic and spirits that are tragic, a kiss for eternal bliss like lightning and static. I sit down here in Devils Creek as the cars drive over the bridge, watching the shadows dance all around as they come down the tree line's ridge. I sit on an old mossy dead tree that fell over a lifetime ago, and when it fell? Who's to tell? If it made a sound? Does no one know? Forgotten tombstones weathered and old, some crumbled away with the stories they told, some still stand, and some are even new, but some people can't even afford a funeral, let alone more than two. Some of these roads to these places I write about have been blocked off and forgotten with time. People don't do the things that they used to when this world used to glow and shine. There was a doppelganger of my former self that would appear here and there out of thin air, but it was me when I describe myself when I'm down here in these stories that I share, appearing here and there and everywhere. I was seeing my own very self as the character in this story, and I wondered when I would appear out of almost seemingly thin air, if anyone else saw me. So I would look around and study other people's reactions to see if anyone else noticed my other self that would seem to disappear and reappear at a whim in the wind whenever I randomly would remember him, and just then a version of myself just as I imagined in the Witchwood Forest and Devils Creek stories would manifest so quickly as if out of thin air that it was mind boggling, and to even more of a shock were people around would indeed react to him and notice him, or should I say me or myself? This reaction by others and the way he would appear and disappear on his or "my" own was a confirmation of the conclusion of these very tales—stories of lost loves, past lives, and longing for the truth and answers of something more, something that felt like a spell or even sometimes dark curses…something that I knew lay just beneath the surface of an illusion that I was reusing long enough to leave scars and bruising in a trip or voyage I was sailing and cruising, stumbling through in an almost state of delusion that was disorientating and confusing.

This is my conclusion. It wasn't just me that was crazy in an ordinary sane and sad world, but something bigger as I was thrown and hurled into. In the spirit of the old clever saying, "It's your world, I'm just living in it," a deeper look at that old comment can show cracks and scratches in the inner dimensional walls of different worlds of existence. Not the universe that offers the same matter and objects that are there when you are not there and still there when you show up as they age with time like our organic bodies that contain our souls but a multiverse that things can appear and reappear as they change at will or at any given time in no particular order. With that being said and a mentioning of the multiverse to feed your imagination, let me take you alongside one of those walls that separate our world from other worlds (worlds such as the spirit world or Valhalla or Helheim). Alongside these walls are ley lines, or to some witch lines. I only need one line to pull you into the conclusion of this tale, a tale that wasn't right, and this line is the fine line between insanity and genius that I would like for you to walk alongside with me. Some people understand a given gift that I am going to pass on to you, and that gift is the current here and now, which is why some people acknowledge the name of here and now being called the present. The present point in time, because with your five or, for some people, six senses and the present point of time, which is here and now is all you have, or for that matter all you really need to be fully aware and alive, which is more than some people ever have, and anything else is material objects. Even the clothes on your back do not really matter, for they, too, are just material matter. Why am I sharing this with you? Because the present is called the present because it is a gift or present to you, and with this gift and your six, or for most people five senses, you become what you perceive now (the gift of present time), you are alive! You are alive and breathing, but how many people truly really know it? You become what you perceive time. However, you perceive time is the reality that you create for yourself.

I'm walking alongside Devils Creek holding on to the tree limbs to prevent from falling off the face of the earth and joining the UFO-littered stars up above into beautiful oblivion. I want to draw down the moon like some ancient druid or pagan ceremony and shape-shift into a bat or raven and fly high into the midnight sky on the very air you breathe, but first I have to tell you something. I have to share with you my conclusion, the drawing down of the moon and stars and elemental night into an ending of this tale that wasn't right, a heart-breaking story that yearns and earns glory, a reason to wake up every dawn and fight. This is a heavy far-out groovy tale that was too deep for most people and way out of sight. I used to dismiss my senses as a failing part of myself, which I also dismissed as a crazy machine in whole. I used to have little to no confidence in myself and was convinced I was simply a batshit crazy mad man and nothing much more. As years pushed on, I began calculating and adding things up, trying my best to make sense out of all the unexplainable things that plagued my life, and soon I started noticing the things that I thought were just a part of my mixed-up mind. My lonely lunatic life was not all as it seemed.

If I was ever in my stages and phases as an atheist or agnostic, then I'd drive myself crazy obsessing over small miracles of God winks dismissed as super coincidences or some other crazy theory because saying, admitting, or believing something more acceptable to most people like a miracle sounded more crazy. So instead of having faith and believing the miracle that was given to me, I'd instead drum up a dozen other more logical explanations that sounded crazier and required even a more crazy mind to understand. Perhaps if it is true when people say "it's all part of God's plan" is. God *wants* just that—for me, you, us, people in general to question these miracles, God winks, and super coincidences to expand our minds and enlighten us. Or perhaps God wants us to challenge these blessings to let us all figure out that alternative explanations only enforce the mind-boggling acceptance that a divine intervention, act, deed, or miracle did indeed take place. It makes me wonder how many times I may have talked to real angels, divine beings, extraterrestrials and didn't even realize it.

How many times have you been bushed by another passerby who may have been battling their own demons? We all have our demons and our skeletons in our dungeon closets. Who knows how many of us may be chasing the dragon with a healthy dose of battling your demonic possessions on the side? To picture a multiverse of other worlds is a sight that is around us in plain view, plain sight almost all the time, but the invention of electric light, as young as it is, has and is and always will sadly be literally fucking with all the animals on earth including us as the human beings. (Humans…a divine, graceful, complicated animal we are. We are beastly and brutal and strong yet graceful, fragile, compassionate, loving creatures.) We are so much different than most animals on earth, evolved in our own unique direction in some way, but because of the light year-ahead mentality, we are too fast-paced for this beautiful ancient world. We are the roman candles that burn bright on both ends, as we self-destruct like a fast-moving plague or cancer on this beautiful graveyard planet of life and death. Our fast-paced thirst for knowledge, power, greed, and dominance has not only sped up our self-destructing demise, but we have managed to suck in our beautiful animals into our bottomless pit of not loving this beautiful planet as well.

We are quicksand that wild animals cannot get too close to; it has only been lately that people started to try to protect our beautiful fellow animals on this earth from going extinct. I know I am getting deep, and perhaps my mind is wandering a little off the drawing conclusion of me and this old creek and why I sit out here in the sound of silence and the nature's sound symphony of nocturnal critters and watching ghosts, spirits, phantoms, and other things that go bump in the night. When you need a visual aid to help you picture a multiverse of other worlds is a sight that is around us in plain view, plain sight almost all the time, and as is it here on this old rotting moss-covered fallen tree log, I am looking at just some of the multiverse we all live in as the world of air shines, flickers, and glimmers and shimmers over my head filled with its frittering screeching bats, its flocks of crows, and looming giant black ravens perched into the outstretched hands of crooked branches swaying across the cold gray moon in these lost forgotten beautiful summer nights. The branches grow out of the land world where I was born onto with all other mankind, men and women whom we all share with the other land-dwelling creeping, stalking, and hunting wolves that follow in the shadows. As the spider contently spins its web in the overhead branches, the giant black rat snake slithers up the treetops to rob a crow's nest of its helpless young. The rotting mossy log I sit on has dead twisted leafless branches dipping into the damp, soggy, wet water world of observant giant alligator snapping turtles and watching slithering, swimming cottonmouth water snakes while the old fat bellied mud cats and alligator gars swim the cold murky bottoms.

I paint a picture that is never too far from you, that is the multiverse that can be observed with your own eyes, where the three worlds of sky, earth, and water all meet. To truly get the wonder of this sight, you must observe the ocean from the banks of a forest. These are just the visual aid to help you understand how more than one world can touch others, and just like the old ley lines and witch lines of the Bermuda Triangle and all the other ley lines crisscrossed and zig-zagged around the world, most other worlds are hard, if not impossible, to be seen with the naked eye. Sometimes we as people feel out of tune or out of balance in a world that we may even feel that we do not belong in. This is why I myself would visit Witchwood Forest and Devils Creek. I felt like I didn't belong, and I needed a secluded lonely place to sit alone and watch the stars as the frogs, crickets, and other insects and birds sang the song of nature's natural symphonies of sweet lullabies. Sometimes the worlds we belong in are not the same one we are currently residing in; perhaps we are just a few adjustments away from a perfect world, just like the picture on your TV set needs to have the tint adjusted and the colors changed a bit. My world was in desperate need of positive adjustments. I was growing tired of carrying a heavy broken heart all alone with no one to help me mend or heal it.

This world was becoming a huge drag and a real bummer. The lack of compassion, mercy, and love had this old space cowboy star gazing in lonesome seclusion, wishing upon lonely shooting stars streaming across the night sky. For all my blessed dear readers who loyally read all my writings, please let these stories wake you up and open your eyes because this is not a game we are playing. This is life. One second, one minute, one hour at a time, the worlds you are sitting on are all spinning underneath you at speeds you could not fathom. The multiverse is, you have only lived your life a small fraction of a microsecond, if that, so embrace every precious second of it. You are a twinkle of a star, as so was she, a little shining star of hope in an ugly dark world. One day I hope to see her again. They do not make 'em like her very often, one of those one-in-a-million type of women that lit up the darkness with an eternal candle and warm flame that could never be extinguished. We are the few, the rarest breeds of human beings that are untouchable on a physical plane but shine like the sun on emotional waves. We met on emotional waves beyond physical planes that the memory saves and plays over and over in frantic reminiscing raves, a handful of the best memories sorted out by the best of our faves. She never died that late night on the side of that country road, but it was me that died as she lived on like a back seat party bong, passed around during a favorite rock 'n' roll song. It was a night that ended terribly horrific for her, but for me it kept on—a night forever long.

Down here in Devils Creek are the painful memories that linger and creep while I fight through the heartache for the truthful answers of the questions I seek. My physical being is gone, and so no matter I can own or keep, just the reasons of memories and feelings I must reap. Ley lines are below my feet as I rise to the shooting stars high above in the infinite night sky; the treetops shrink as my soul rises, as if I could fly. Down below is Devils Creek and Witchwood Forest. The answers I was scared to face have finally set me free from this place. How long have I lingered here while lifetimes have slowly aged the old trees, widening them too big to wrap arms around the forgotten moss-covered trunks. Down there was a region I let go to no longer ever retrieve, I drift farther away from the legions of forest spirits behind me, I finally leave. Our energy that we all carry, our tiny souls in our huge bodies are no longer weird or scary; the answers are all so strange and freaky, but facing and accepting them lets me escape this place that can no longer keep me. Look to the muddy banks of Devils Creek and you will see my footsteps next to yours, time's muddy waters floods and washes them from the shores.

Smiles and laughter she loves and adores are distant memories the mind no longer stores high above. With me, the ravens and blackbirds quietly soars on summer night winds, and tiny headlights below go somewhere unrelated and outdated. We got away and made it to our destination; beautiful destiny holds fates with no hesitation. I'm just a kid at heart. We all should hold on to our inner children selves within while years of aging carries us to the new world that is waiting disguised as the end. People forget as they weep tears of sorrow, to embrace the gothic darkness to unlock the doors of tomorrow. Scared to feel pain, go insane, lonely, depressed, and hollow, people ignore, guilt, and shame. Scared to lead the way, they grow bitter and shallow, wasting precious time as they only follow. I'm leaving it all behind, with no particular or specific time, under the lunar glow of the full moon shine. I learned a lot from these thoughts and feelings deep inside. I bid you all a farewell with the words, "It has been one enchanting magical ride." Time to let go, move on, learn and grow, test out all the things I feel and know…to a whole new world we all must eventually go.

The End

ABOUT THE AUTHOR

DANIEL "DEVIL JAMES" Burrus, aka Danny Boy, is a legendary eccentric from the back country roads of rural Illinois. He grew up in the shadow of the big city of St. Louis in a little town about twenty-eight miles east of the mighty Mississippi River called Highland Illinois, where he left quite a mark among the locals as what they would call a wild man of the let-it-all-hang-out standards in the key of "let your freak flag fly." In and out of jails, rehabs, mental institutions, he fought for the right to dance proudly to the beat of his own drum rather than conforming and living a life that he despised early on. He's traveled the world and battled drug and alcohol addiction, homelessness, and so much more. Much like a fallen archangel who held on to the precious moral compass of life, he earned back his graceful ranks among the divine with his much loved collectible paintings, poetry, stories, music, and spoken word. His art became an underground cult following and spread quickly with fans abroad. Daniel has always left a lasting impression on all those who met or knew him not only for his abstract, eccentric way of thinking and his unique kindness but also for his ability to always be thought-provoking and inspiring in a rattle-your-cage type of way. Daniel currently lives in the tiny country town of Trenton, Illinois, just a country mile from his hometown highland, where he has finally discovered a surreal life of contentment living clean and sober with a humble philosophic state of being. We can only hope and pray that he will stay this way.